Right
To My
Wrong

Book 8 of The Heroes of The Dixie Wardens MC

LANI LYNN VALE

Copyright © 2015 Lani Lynn Vale

**ISBN-13:
978-1523377800**

**ISBN-10:
1523377801**

Dedication\

These are always so hard for me to write. Everyone I love knows this wouldn't be possible without them. My husband. My kids. My mom. My sister. My mother in law. Everyone that is always there for me...you mean the world to me. <3 y'all!

Acknowledgements

FuriousFotog- AKA Golden. You keep taking these beautiful photos, and I'll keep buying them.

Chase Ketron- The same goes for you. Before long I'm going to have a library all with you on the cover. :)

CONTENTS

Other Titles by Lani Lynn Vale:
The Freebirds

Boomtown

Highway Don't Care

Another One Bites the Dust

Last Day of My Life

Texas Tornado

I Don't Dance

The Heroes of The Dixie Wardens MC

Lights To My Siren

Halligan To My Axe

Kevlar To My Vest

Keys To My Cuffs

Life To My Flight

Charge To My Line

Code 11- KPD SWAT Series

Center Mass

Double Tap

Bang Switch

Execution Style

Charlie Foxtrot

Kill Shot

Coup De Grace

PROLOGUE

It's said that birthmarks are where you were killed in your previous life. Apparently I was killed by someone stabbing me in my boob. What a bitch way to die!
-Ruthie's secret thoughts

Ruthie

"So, what's your story?" The man at my side asked me.

I looked up from peeling the label off my beer and stared at him.

He was so beautiful, but everything I would never go for again.

Muscular.

Military.

An Alpha.

Those three things combined made for a man who always felt he knew the right way.

"What do you mean, what's my story?" I muttered, looking back towards my label.

"Where'd you grow up?" He was a persistent bastard.

"Typical shit upbringing. My dad left my mom. My mom felt the benefits of having me were outweighed by the negatives of having me, so she gave me up for adoption. I never found anyone to take me in, so I spent twelve years in the foster system. When I turned eighteen, I was kicked out on the street, and I did the only thing I could, found a man that could support me. But he also liked to hit me. After a year of that, I killed him," I said softly.

7

If knowing that fact was going to scare him off, I wanted to get it over with before I made a friend out of him. I wasn't a fan of false niceties. I was a rip the band aid off kind of girl.

"Sawyer said you just got out," the man continued.

I sighed and finally looked at him.

He was handsome.

So handsome that it was making me tongue tied. I wasn't hot like most of the other women in the room. I was decent looking, but I wasn't in his league.

Which was why I was looking at the label of my beer the majority of the time instead of at his face.

He'd been sitting beside me ever since I'd sat down, and I couldn't figure out why.

In fact, he was downright gorgeous. Everything that made him wrong.

And the beard just made it even worse.

I couldn't resist a beard.

Never could…and never would.

Tall with muscular arms. Wide shoulders. Deep green eyes and a messy mop of dirty blonde hair tumbling over his eyes, he was every woman's dream.

His beard was one of those that was grown out of necessity instead of style, the kind where you were out in the desert and not near a razor kind of beard.

Which was conducive with the party we were having in honor of him coming home from his deployment in Afghanistan.

"Do you want me to leave you alone, because I'm sensing that from you," the man said.

I sighed and looked at him, caught by those beautiful green eyes.

"Sterling, I'm one fucked up mess," I finally said.

He grinned. "Well that makes two of us. I'm a fucked up mess molded into a ball of denial. Trust me. My fucked up mess could easily compete with your fucked up mess."

I laughed.

If only that were true.

CHAPTER 1

Sometimes people are too chatty in the morning. And according to the Coffee Gods, it's okay to kill those people. Slowly.
-Ruthie's secret thoughts

Ruthie

"Shit, fuck, shit fucking hell," I growled as I ran from my car to the convenience store where I worked.

The convenience store was one of three in the city of Benton, Louisiana, and I happened to work at the one in the harsher side of town.

But I liked it.

My boss gave me the hours I wanted.

I could go to school, and I could still work at my other job at Halligans and Handcuffs, seeing as it was the job that made me the most money.

Sterling and his three brothers, foster care brothers not club member brothers, came in every three days before they worked out.

Each would grab an energy drink. A Monster for Sterling, and Nos for his two brothers, and two Gatorade's a piece. Only ever in the red. No blue, orange, or yellow for those guys.

Then they'd take turns paying.

I'd gathered over the last half a year that the middle brother was a baseball player, and the other two supported him during workouts and practice.

Or, at least, when Sterling was here, he did.

He'd been deployed about five months ago, and had just returned two weeks ago.

And I'd missed my time to see him if I didn't hurry!

Shit!

I stepped in a puddle of water, saturating my pants leg all the way up to my knee.

"Dammit," I growled, hitching my bag over my shoulder once more and walking quickly.

I didn't run, though.

Not once I hit the slick black top near the pumps.

It always seemed to gather oil and the likes, and when it rained, it became like a slip and slide.

I'd seen no less than fifteen people bust their asses over the last six months that I'd worked there.

I'd told my boss that it was a hazard and that one day someone would sue, but all he could say to that was, 'Let them. Then they can have this place and I wouldn't have to deal with my mother in law anymore.'

I breathed a sigh of relief when my feet hit the sidewalk that would lead me inside the store, and shivered violently when a bolt of lightning came down out of the sky and seemed to practically touch the tip of a six foot pole that was just to the left of where I'd parked my car.

"Holy hell," I said in awe.

I'd always been interested in meteorology. I was just not smart enough to go that route when I had the chance.

At thirty two, I was well on the way to middle aged, and there just wasn't time to go anywhere in life anymore.

"You're late!" My boss, Dane, growled at my side.

I gasped and jumped, covering my face in reflex.

Not because I thought he'd hit me, but because it was simply just a reaction.

Something that'd been ingrained in me since I was a young kid living in a foster home full of kids that liked to beat you up for the hell of it.

Dane didn't take offense to my maneuverings, only nodded at me, staying where he was so he wouldn't scare me anymore than he already had.

"Hey," I said. "My car's a bitch in the rain."

Dane smiled. "You should get a new one. You can afford it now."

I could. But I didn't want to waste my hard earned money that I was saving to buy a house on a car. That wouldn't be practical.

I mean, I already had a car that worked. What was the point in getting something new?

"I know, I know. You've been telling me that every day for a month. I just don't want to get a new car," I said. "I'm saving up for a house."

In reality, I was saving up for a house that I could pay outright, seeing as everyone in this stupid town thought that I wasn't good enough to be here.

Apparently, they looked upon a convicted killer with vehemence.

My husband, Bender, had been a real asshole.

He liked to beat me when he drank.

Beat me when he didn't drink.

Beat me when he was mad.

Beat me when I looked at him funny.

Beat me when I forgot to wash his uniform.

If you could think it up, Bender beat me for it.

He literally hated everything about me.

But he'd knocked me up when I was eighteen, and his parents had made him 'do the right thing.'

And he'd *hated* that.

He wanted to marry another woman. Had had his sights on Lily Brianne, my best friend since I was twelve.

I hadn't known that, though.

Lily and I had gone through a lot together.

We'd been in the same foster home until we were eighteen and kicked out since our foster mother was no longer under any obligations to allow us to stay there. Plus, she wasn't getting any more money for us, so what was the point?

I stowed my things in the locker, and headed to the front counter and thought about Lily and me.

Lily and I had moved into a women's shelter in Monroe, Louisiana the same night we landed in Monroe.

We'd started working shortly after that, and then we shared a one bedroom apartment.

Then we started going to school, where we met Bender.

Well, we'd met Bender before, of course. We'd all gone to the same high school. Bender had qualified for a full scholarship at the same college we had randomly picked to attend.

Yet, we were in such different social circles that we never got a second look from Bender and his peers

Or so we thought.

Lily obviously got a lot more attention from Bender than I did.

Bender got a lot more attention from me rather than Lily, who had her sights set on another man at our college. Bender's best friend.

And Bender hated that. Absolutely *hated* it.

So he moved to little old me in hopes that he'd catch the attention of Lily.

I, of course, didn't know that at the time.

I was too busy being on top of the world that the man that I was half in love with was giving me the time of day.

Too young and eager to please, I slept with him on the first date.

He left once he realized that the tactic wasn't going to work with Lily.

He never spoke to me again until six weeks later when I told him that I was pregnant.

I still wasn't sure how his parents had found out.

Whatever the reason, I'd been done with him because I wasn't into trapping men.

But I had had a difficult pregnancy at the beginning.

Medical bills started piling up.

And then Bender's parents got involved, forcing us to marry.

The bell above the door rang, and I looked up, smiling at the man that came through the door.

"If it isn't Mr. Baseball!" I crowed.

Sterling flipped me off.

"You've got the wrong guy; that dumbass is behind me," he said. "I'm just helping him look the part."

"I take offense to that, you big dick muncher," a voice said from just behind Sterling.

I stood on my tip toes to see his two brothers following close behind him.

Cormac was the 'baseball' player.

He was about a month away from starting his final season of baseball at ULM.

The University of Louisiana of Monroe was lucky to have him, from what I'd heard.

He was older than all the other players, at twenty five, having not started attending college until he was twenty one.

Cormac was six foot of lean muscle and sinew with black hair and a quick smile.

Their other brother, Garrison, was the same age as Cormac.

Although that's about where the similarities ended.

Garrison wasn't what I would call 'cute.'

He was too mean looking to be called cute.

He had a perpetual scowl on his face that rarely could be seen through his bushy beard.

He was in shape, though.

Very good shape.

He'd have to be to keep up with the other two.

He was currently a high school science teacher and baseball coach for Shreveport High School, and probably the most feared man in the school.

I would've shit myself had I been sent to the office to have to deal with him.

But he really was loved.

He was a sweet man, from what little I'd spoken to him at Halligans and Handcuffs and here.

But my heart belonged to the man that came up to the counter to talk to me instead of grabbing his drinks.

"How ya been?" He asked.

I smiled at what I now counted as one of my best friends in the world.

"My car doesn't like the rain. I think I need new tires or something. They wouldn't grip the pavement for nothing," I said, shaking my head and reaching behind the counter for a package of sunflower seeds I kept back there especially for him.

Dane didn't like selling sunflower seeds.

I didn't know why, and I didn't ask.

But I bought them at the Sam's store and brought them up here every day for him.

He smiled and shoved the package into his front pocket.

My eyes followed the movement, mouthwatering as I watched the front of his elastic shorts dip down, exposing the taut side of his stomach before disappearing once again as his hand came out of his pocket.

"Wanna play a game of baseball with us this evening?" He asked.

He asked me every time.

And every time I told him no.

Not because I wasn't good at baseball, but because I *was*. Well, softball, anyway.

It brought back memories that hurt.

Memories of Lily and me when we were happy.

Before anything Bender related ever happened to us.

"What will you give me if I play?" I asked, surprising not just myself, but him as well.

"A ride?" He answered helpfully.

I laughed. "Why do you do all these baseball games, anyway?"

"Because it's easier to see where Cormac is and keep him ready for anything," he explained.

I wanted to roll my eyes.

"What you guys do isn't what I would call a game. It's a bunch of guys drinking beer, while the women watch from the sidelines cheering their men on," I challenged.

He grinned, and his eyes glowed with happiness.

If times were different...if life was different...Sterling and I might have been able to pursue what I could feel between us.

But times *weren't* different, and my life *wasn't* all shits and giggles like Sterling needed.

I had demons.

I had so many demons that it was a wonder I functioned at all.

And Sterling deserved a woman that would stand by his side, make him proud to have his arm around her.

And I wasn't that woman.

So I made a promise to myself, while staring at that smile. A promise that I wouldn't drag Sterling down with me.

He wouldn't get caught up in me and everything that floated around me like a hurricane ready to destroy anyone that entered my proximity.

"Regardless of what it is, I want you to come. I know you used to play.

And we could use some new blood," he said. "I'll pick you up at six."

I blinked as I watched him throw a twenty on the counter as all three men walked out only moments later, bickering about someone having the 'hots' for a woman that was way too straight laced to ever date him.

I had a feeling they were speaking about me, but that couldn't be further from the truth.

Sterling didn't deserve to have to deal with my crap.

Not even a little bit.

"Now that you've had your fun, how about you get your shit together and go clean the bathroom," Dane ordered.

I smiled at Dane.

He was a great boss.

He knew I had a secret crush on Sterling.

Knew it and loved to tease me about it.

"What's wrong with Allison doing it like she usually does?" I asked, walking around the counter to grab the mop bucket out of the storage closet.

"Allison called in sick because she thinks she has the flu," he said. "So it's just you and me this week, chicka."

Yay!

Not.

That would suck.

If it was just me and him, that'd mean that I would be needed for more hours, which would hack in to my nap time.

"Just don't expect me to work tonight or tomorrow night. And Friday night. I have plans tonight, and the bar the other two nights," I told him.

Dane nodded. "I know. I was listening to that boy try to ask you out."

I smiled.

"He wasn't trying to ask me out."

Dane gave me a look.

"Honey, I have a dick. I know what it looks like when a guy's dick is hard. And his was hard. For you. Trust me," he said, sitting down on the stool behind the register and turning his eyes to the TV screen that was sitting next to the register.

Rolling my eyes, I rolled the mop into the bathroom and started the tedious job of cleaning up the bathroom.

The girl's was never that bad.

It was the men's that always got me.

How could grown men miss the toilet like that?

By the time I was done with the men's bathroom, I felt the need for a hot shower and a beer. Both of which I couldn't have right then…and since I had somewhere to go later, I wouldn't be having it for a very long time.

But just the thought of seeing Sterling again made my heart race.

"Your phone's been ringing the whole time you were in there," Dane said as he shoved three cheese crackers into his mouth.

I rolled my eyes.

Why wouldn't it have occurred to him that I needed to answer that call if they called that many times?

I smiled when I saw Lily's smiling face lighting up the screen of my phone.

"Hello?" Lily answered breathlessly.

"Hey! What'd you need?" I asked.

Lily called once a day regardless of if she 'needed' anything or not.

It was just who we were.

And I'd missed her constantly when I was locked up.

"I have someone who wanted to talk to you before you she went on stage," she said happily.

I smiled as Lily's daughter, Toni, got on the phone.

"Aunt Ruthie, guess what!" Toni yelled loudly.

I looked down at my hands and smiled through the pain.

"What, stinker bell?" I asked softly.

"I hit a home run today at Putt-Putt!" She squealed.

I smiled, my pain taking a backseat to the excitement in Toni's voice.

See, Toni and my daughter, Jade, would've been the same age right then.

But my husband had nearly beaten me to death when I was almost eight months pregnant, and I'd lost my baby girl before I'd ever even held her.

Lily had found out she was pregnant the week before I'd lost my little Jade, and it was heart breaking to talk to Toni when I couldn't talk to my own little girl that would've been doing something similar had she been able to live.

"Don't you mean hole in one?" I asked her, a smile in my voice.

I could practically see her shaking her head when she replied.

"No. I mean, daddy tossed me the ball, and I hit it with my golf club. And I hit the ball into the last hole at the very end of the course," she corrected me.

I closed my eyes. "Your daddy should know better."

"See," Lily said as she came back on the line. "That's what I said. He's like a big two year old."

I smiled at my hands.

Dante was such a good guy.

He started an auto recovery business when he got out of the Air Force and, from what I'd heard, was a pretty successful businessman now.

He had my whole heart, though.

He was such a good man, always there for me if I needed him to be.

He'd come to visit me when Lily made the trip.

He was a good father and a good friend.

Something that I desperately wished I had married instead of the man I had.

"So where are you going?" I asked, ringing up a man's purchase as I did so.

The man gave me a funny look since I was on the phone, but I ignored him, stuffing things into the bag as I held the phone in between my ear and shoulder.

"Nine fifty seven," I said.

The man gave me a credit card and I swiped it through the card reader before handing it back to him while listening to Lily tell me about Toni's recital that was scheduled to take place in twenty minutes.

"You're late," I laughed. "Shouldn't you have left already?"

I handed the man his receipt and he took it with a slight huff of annoyance.

"Yeah, about twenty minute ago. But we were having a meltdown because we couldn't find the pink shoes, only the blue shoes," Lily said. "We only found a single pink one, so now we're wearing one blue and one pink."

"Well, that works," I laughed.

And it did.

What little girl wanted to wear blue shoes when she could wear pink?

"Alright, gotta go. I love you," Lily said as she hung up the phone.

I rolled my eyes and shoved the phone into my back pocket before turning to Dane.

"What's up with you?" I asked.

Dane smiled.

"Well, I have a prostate exam around four, and I have a colonoscopy next Tuesday that they're going to make me shit..."

I stopped him.

"That's enough information, Dane. Thanks, though."

He shrugged.

"Well, you were the one who asked."

That I did.

And I would not be asking anymore.

***

I walked out of my house that I was renting, into the late afternoon sun, annoyed and unbelievably pissed off.

"What's that look for?" Sterling asked me.

I handed him the ticket I'd received.

"I got a ticket for a boat parked in front of my house that isn't even mine," I told him, walking to the passenger seat and hopping inside without prompting.

My neighbors hated me.

Literally *hated* me.

I was in a house that I'd rented through the chief of police.

It was nice to have a hookup through my other best friend, Sawyer.

She was currently married to the president of a motorcycle club.

The same club that Sterling belonged to.

Sterling wasn't wearing his cut, or the leather biker vest that he usually wore, delineating him a member of The Dixie Wardens MC.

But I guessed it probably wasn't the most comfortable thing to wear when you were outside working out in one hundred degree weather.

"So whose boat is it if it's not yours?" Sterling asked from my open window.

I pointed at the man across the street sipping his beer with his feet up on the porch railing.

"That man's," I pointed at him.

Sterling looked at him, hunching down so he could see through the truck's open windows, and grimaced.

"Hold on," he said. "Be right back."

I shrugged.

I'd already tried talking to the man, but he was a dick, so I just left.

I was planning on going up to the police station tomorrow and talk it out to whomever would listen, but if Sterling wanted to try that for me, then I'd let him.

I had enough on my plate to deal with without something minor like this.

I watched and sipped on my ice water through my Camelback water bottle that cost way too much money for me to own so many.

Sterling topped the man's front steps and crossed his arms.

I could see his mouth moving, but other than that, couldn't make out what was being said.

However, by the tension in the man's previously loose shoulders, I could tell that whatever was being said wasn't very nice.

Or appealing to the older man.

"That's where I've always parked my boat!" The man yelled.

Sterling said something calmly to the man, and the man reluctantly took the ticket that Sterling held out to him, ripping it from Sterling's hands and shoving it down into his pocket.

I blinked, and then blinked some more, as I watched Sterling come down the steps and straight to his truck.

He got into his side, slammed the door, and started the engine up with a dull roar.

Seconds later, he was driving away from the curb before he explained.

"The man's going to move the boat tomorrow. And he's going to go take care of your ticket," he said without hesitation.

"That's awesome. I can't believe he was just going to let me pay it, though. I mean, who does that?" I asked.

He shrugged. "No clue."

"Not sure why you'd even get a ticket for that. Seems inconsequential seeing as they had two murders in the city last night," Sterling said, shaking his head.

Not knowing what to say to that, I asked, "Why aren't you on your bike?"

He grinned as he turned to me, glancing quickly before he turned back to the road.

"It's hard to carry a bat bag, balls, and plates in your saddle bags," he said.

Ahh, that made sense.

"Huh," I said. "So when do you go back?"

I didn't have to explain what I meant by 'go back.'

He knew exactly what I meant.

"I have to be back in Belle Chasse in another thirteen days," he answered as he swung the wheel wide to get out of my neighborhood.

My mouth dropped open. "You're already going back that quick?"

He nodded. "Yeah, but I'm not getting deployed, at least. I'll be there for about three months while they decide what to do with us next. Normally we would be heading to California, so I'm lucky they're allowing us to do it so close to home."

I just shook my head.

I just got him back!

"How often will you come back?" I asked softly.

I was fairly sure I was hiding my sadness well, but he placed his hand on top of mine where it rested between us on the seat.

His big fingers forced themselves in between mine as he said, "I'll probably be back every weekend. Gotta get my boy ready for baseball. And I have a vested interest in someone special."

I blinked, suddenly hurt.

He had a 'vested interest' in somebody?

What was that supposed to mean?

Was he seeing somebody?

I didn't get the answer before we pulled into the ball park's parking lot.

We were playing on the city's baseball field where the upper age's played.

It was a normal sized ball field for baseball, and it was absolutely massive.

The back fence went about as far out as a regulation major league field, which was a big thing for this little town.

Especially when the only single person to be able to hit it over the center back wall was currently walking beside me onto the field.

"So did you really hit that ball, or was it one of those infield homerun's because it bounced over the fence?" I teased.

I knew it was really a hit.

I'd watched the YouTube video of it.

It'd been a huge thing for this small town, especially since Sterling and his Dixie Youth baseball team had put the small town on the map.

Sterling's team, The Wildcat's, had been down by three points in the bottom of the ninth with Sterling up to bat.

He'd gotten two strikes, three balls, and was in the final pitch when he hit a foul.

He did that four more times before he finally connected.

And connect he fucking did.

It was amazing.

One of the sweetest hits I'd ever witnessed.

Something you'd never expect from an eighteen year old.

The ball had gone over the fence, dead center, and Sterling had gone around the bases with a look of awe on his face.

The video had ended with the entire team, as well as many of the fans, dog piling Sterling.

Now, seven years later, his name was still plastered at the top of the scoreboard next to all the other boys who went to the World's that year.

"There was no bounce whatsoever, trust me. I hit that fucker so hard that it reverberated through my body and centered in my heart," he told me solemnly. "I can still feel the way the bat and ball connected."

"It was fucking perfection!" Cormac crowed. "I've never witnessed something so great in my life!"

The animation in Cormac's voice had everyone around us laughing, and I smiled at the man at my side.

"Seems you have a fan," I surmised.

He nodded. "The biggest."

Cormac grinned and bent down to grab the glove and ball at his feet.

"Let's play ball!"

CHAPTER 2

*Wrong. Your mother is wrong. Your face is wrong. Everything
about you is wrong.
-Ruthie's secret thoughts*

Ruthie

"Oh my God," I said into my pillow.

"What's wrong with you?" Sawyer said from the foot of my bed.

I didn't scream like I wanted to.

I knew she was there…well, at least knew she was in my house.

I hadn't realized she was that close, though.

"I can't move," I whispered. "I think I'm paralyzed."

"You played really awesome, if it's any consolation," she said, bouncing
on the bed a few times.

I glared over at my cute pregnant friend.

"Why are you here? It's my day off," I grumbled, turning over and
yanking the blanket over me.

Or would have had it not been partially under Sawyer's ass.

"You promised me you'd go to help me register for the baby shower,"
she told me.

I groaned. "I meant that in a lying kind of way. The kind of thing where
you say niceties, yet don't follow through with them because you know
you don't really want to do it."

"Well, you said it and I'm not letting you take it back," she grumbled. "Get up. I'm making eggs."

"I don't like eggs," I muttered to the now empty room.

How did a pregnant woman have so much energy?

Shouldn't they be tired all the time? Because I hadn't seen that from Sawyer yet so far, and she was well into her seventh month.

Rolling out of bed, very painfully, I walked blindly to the bathroom, only opening my eyes a crack to give me a hint of where I was going.

I left the light off as I took care of business, brushed my teeth, and walked out into the main room.

It didn't even occur to me that there'd be anyone else there, which was why when I finally opened my bleary eyes and saw the tall, sexy man sitting on my couch talking to Sawyer, I froze.

"Uh," Sawyer said, finally seeing me. "You could've put some pants on."

I could hear the laughter in her voice as she said it, and I wanted to smack that smile off her face.

I flipped her off and turned on my heel, walking back to the bedroom and pulling on a pair of sweatpants I had on top of my clean pile.

Being in my panties next to Sawyer really wasn't that big of a deal.

We'd lost any and all dignity during our time in prison, so it wasn't a surprise that I'd walk out there with no pants on.

Hell, we'd peed next to each other for eight years.

Vomited. Shit. Saw each other naked.

There was nothing sacred between us.

But she could've at least shouted a warning that she'd let someone into my house!

I came back out glaring at the two people on my couch.

"Where's breakfast?" I mumbled darkly.

Sawyer smiled.

She'd been the morning person.

I'd been the afternoon and night person.

It was incredibly annoying to be paired with that type of person, but I learned to cherish her nonetheless.

"I got sidetracked," she said, pointing to Sterling.

Sterling grinned at her and stood, reaching into his pocket for something.

"I brought you your glove and wallet back. You left them in my truck last night," he said, pointing to glove and wallet before pulling out a piece of paper. "But then I saw this parked on your car, and I felt the need to call Loki."

I looked at the paper he held out to me like it was a live snake, instead focusing on the fact that he'd called another police officer to my house.

Loki was another member of The Dixie Wardens.

He was the scary one of the bunch.

His blonde hair was cut close to his scalp, and his eyes were hard.

Cop eyes hard.

But the defining factor that made him scarier than the rest was the scar across his throat.

I'd only heard bits and pieces of how he got it, but from what I'd gathered from all of them, it was because of a gang initiation or something.

But it was the way he watched me that made me the most nervous.

Almost as if he could tell I was a bad person.

And I guess most would think I was, but I wasn't.

I was only protecting myself…and my unborn child that didn't make it.

Not that anybody besides me and Sawyer knew about my Jade.

I hadn't even told Lily about Jade.

Not because I didn't feel that she would sympathize, but because the fact that I'd lost her still hurt so deeply that I couldn't talk about it.

Hadn't talked about it since the day she was taken from me after I spoke to the cops.

"Wonderful," I muttered, turning on my heel to walk into the kitchen and start a pot of coffee.

But it was already done when I got there, so I guess Sawyer was a smidge off the hook.

I didn't bother with cream.

This was a straight black kind of day.

I grimaced when I took a drink of the bitter brew, turning to survey Sawyer and Sterling.

They had a good relationship, but Sawyer had that with all of The Dixie Wardens.

A perk, I guessed, of being with the President.

"How do you still not know what you're having?" Sterling asked my best friend. "Isn't that something new parents want to know?"

I'd asked the same thing.

How do you have a baby shower if you don't know what you're having?

You won't want to put your kid in yellow for that long, not when there's way cuter things in blue or pink.

But she'd refused.

She wanted it to 'be a surprise.'

Something she echoed to Sterling moments later.

"I want it to be a surprise. Silas' doesn't care, but I do. I want that experience since I'm fairly positive this'll be my only one," she admitted.

That was news to me.

I always saw Sawyer as having five children and a minivan.

Silas, I saw, giving her whatever the hell she wanted, and if it was five kids, then he'd do it.

Willingly.

"Why do you say it's your only one?" Sterling asked, leaning his slim hips up against the counter.

My eyes went down to the bulge in the back of his jeans that meant he was carrying.

Something that nearly every man that was a member of The Dixie Wardens did, every single time I saw them.

Sterling being no different.

"Because Silas is older than me. And I don't think he wants anymore kids," she said hesitantly.

I blinked, surprised by that.

"You think that, really? I always figured him for being wrapped around your finger. Ask him and see what he wants," I told her.

Sterling nodded. "I agree with grumpy."

I glared at him. "I'm not grumpy."

He gave me a raised brow, then his eyes moved lower to my breasts.

My gaze followed his to see the Dwarf on my shirt, Grumpy.

Hmmm, maybe I shouldn't have worn this one. Not to mention I didn't even have a bra on yet.

I moved my glare back to his face to see him smiling at my discomfort, and my nipples started to bead in anticipation. Shit but the man really was sexy.

The perfect example of a military man from the tips of his combat boots to the length of his beard.

I licked my lips as my eyes settled on his mouth, and snapped my gaze away from him.

"Breakfast?" I blurted, trying to get away from that knowing smile.

Sawyer nodded and walked to my fridge where she pulled out a gallon of orange juice, and a package of groceries that contained eggs, sausage, and canned biscuits.

She really was laying it on thick if she was going to go that far out of her way to make sure I was fed.

"What kind of eggs do you like, Sterling?" she asked as she placed the bags onto the counter.

"Over easy," he said oddly, almost as if he wasn't aware that there were any other types to eat in the morning.

Sawyer nodded as she started to pull out a frying pan from somewhere I'd never seen before, followed up with a pan from above my stove.

I narrowed my eyes.

Had she gone shopping?

Because I definitely would've remembered having either of those items.

I hadn't cooked since I'd moved in unless it was microwavable, and I was fairly certain I had a pot *only*.

"Where'd that come from?" I asked her suspiciously.

"I found it at a yard sale," she lied.

I narrowed my eyes and went to her purse, pulling out receipt after receipt.

My eyes scanned for it and I found it at the very bottom.

"You lying whore!" I yelled, waving the receipt around.

She shrugged.

"At one point, you're going to need to get a pot and a pan. It's not my fault you won't get one. When I come over to cook, I want something to work with!" Sawyer yelled right back.

I glared at her.

"You need to leave me alone! And I never asked you to cook!" I pointed at her.

She ignored me though while she started to place the bacon in the frying pan.

I narrowed my eyes at her and walked into the kitchen, picking up the tube of biscuits and peeling the paper off of it.

Before I'd gotten it all the way off, it exploded in my hand and I shrieked.

"Fuck!" I yelled.

"Serves you right, hoe," Sawyer muttered under her breath.

I flipped her off, ignoring the man that was at my back laughing at our back and forth banter.

I put the biscuits onto the pan and Sawyer stopped me.

"You need cooking spray," she said, freezing me.

"Why would you need cooking spray when these are made with these butter pieces things? Aren't they naturally lubricating?" I asked her, ignoring the fact that she wanted me to spray butter on the pan.

"Are you asking me if you can use butter for lube, seriously?" Sawyer asked in exasperation, moving away from the now popping bacon to the pan where she picked up every single one of the biscuits and sprayed the sheet down before placing them back.

"Seriously?" I asked her.

She glared at me.

"Go sit down. You're interrupting my flow," she hissed.

I washed my hands in the sink and sat down at the island next to Sterling, ignoring the smile on his face.

"So, what are you doing today?" he asked me.

I sighed.

"Apparently going to the baby store and registering for things she doesn't need," I told him.

He snorted.

"You could come play baseball with me," he offered.

I snorted and stood, turning slightly so he could see my side when I lifted my shirt.

He winced.

I'd been hit yesterday by Cormac, of all people, and the ball had struck me in the lower ribs on my back.

I felt Sterling trace around my bruise with one finger, encircling the entire thing before he said, "It looks pretty bad. I can't believe he hurt you."

I laughed. "But I got a walk out of it."

He winked. "Guess if that was worth it for you."

It was.

They threw really hard, not caring that I was a girl.

Or that the other men playing with us hadn't played baseball like they had.

So I was happy for the walk, because stealing bases was where it was at for me, hence why I now had huge scrapes on my ass from stealing bases.

Which was where Sterling went next.

"Your ass was pretty raw," he said.

I nodded, remembering he'd seen it as I'd walked out of the room earlier.

"I'm pretty sore," I admitted.

He nodded. "You're gonna need some sliding pants if you keep coming with us."

I smiled. "I had some before, but I haven't been able to find them since I've gotten all of my stuff. Not that I've really had the reason to really look for them. It was only a cursory skim through them before you showed up yesterday."

He nodded. "Do you have to work today?"

I nodded. "At Halligans and Handcuffs."

He smiled. "Then I'll see you there."

I turned my head to stare at him.

"Why?"

He didn't usually hang out there, at least not when I'd seen him.

He usually had his time spoken for, doing odds and ends for the club, or hanging out with Garrison or Cormac.

There were also a lot of women happy to see him home, too.

Sadly, my radar wasn't the only one he was clocking on.

"There's a party there later," he answered. "We're celebrating Sebastian's birthday."

I blinked.

"Really? No one told me," I said. "Do I even have to work?"

He shrugged. "Shit if I know. All I know is that we're supposed to be there for a 'surprise' at ten until seven."

I frowned.

"Well, I guess I'll just go, and if I'm not needed, I'll head home," I said, thinking about what I would do without the day's tips.

It was already a tight squeeze with them, without them might leave me short on the new clothes I'd intended to buy.

"Shit," Sawyer said.

I looked over to her to see she dropped a piece of bacon, and looked around for her dog, but didn't see him.

"Where is your dog at?" I asked Sawyer suddenly.

Normally we took him everywhere with us, especially since he was being trained as a service dog by Sawyer.

There was no way to acclimate him to new experiences if he didn't go with her to experience them.

She grimaced.

"They have him at the vet to be neutered," she answered.

I winced.

That'd been a bone of contention between Silas and Sawyer for a while now.

She didn't want to get it done and he did.

She wanted her dog, Yogi, to be able to have puppies if he wanted to, and Silas was tired of him pissing all over their house.

His hope was by getting him neutered, he'd stop pissing a 'river in their goddamn kitchen.'

"So he finally talked you into it?" I asked with a laugh.

"There was no 'talking.' Only him 'telling.' Trust me, I tried really hard to free him, but Silas was gone before I woke up this morning," she pouted.

Sterling snorted.

"When we walked into the house yesterday around noon, Yogi had pissed from the front door all the way to the back door," Sterling told her.

Sawyer winced.

I, on the other hand, thought that was quite impressive.

Especially since he had to go through a hallway, past the living room through the kitchen and dining room before coming to a stop at the back door.

Talk about talent!

"Yeah, that's why he's being gelded today," she answered. "I had to listen to that all night long. He's already pissed that I get down on my knees too much."

I snorted coffee into my nose, then started laughing as I pictured a man like Silas *ever* complaining about her being on her knees too much.

Sterling pounded me on the back to help with my breathing, I assumed, but it only ended up making me less able to breathe due to his nearness.

"Loki's here," I mumbled as I heard a bike pull up outside.

I was using anything I could to get the man's hand off me.

Because I might spontaneously burst into orgasm right here next to him, and holy hell would that be embarrassing!

"I'll get the door and let him in," Sterling mumbled as he slipped from his seat.

Once he disappeared from my sight I turned to study Sawyer.

"You doing okay?" I asked her, really looking at her now.

She had a fake smile pasted on her face, the kind that were always meant to make her look 'fine.'

However, I knew her.

I knew everything about her down to the very last detail.

I knew when she was getting sick, or getting her period.

I knew when she was having a bad day because the guards were being douche bags, or another woman was fucking with her.

I knew her.

She was my girl, the only person that I trusted all of my secrets to.

Except one, I thought morosely.

But it wasn't like I was trying to keep that one from her.

It was just too hard to talk about it.

I'd be better showing it to her.

An idea started to form in my mind, and I smiled down at my plate when I realized just what exactly I could do.

"I'm having a bad day," Sawyer mumbled, snapping my attention away from myself and to her.

"Why?" I asked her.

She shrugged.

"Went to the store to get this food, and saw a couple of women who thought it'd be funny to make fun of me. That's all." She shifted and looked away like it was no big deal.

Anger pierced my chest, sharp and tight.

Those fucking women!

Seriously, that was all this town did was gossip about us!

What was the big damn deal?

So we were in prison?

Big deal.

Millions of people every year are in prison for something or another, yet these stuffy women weren't talking about *them*.

Cops were being killed all over the country.

A war was going on the other side of the world.

Children were going hungry.

Animals were being abused.

Seriously, there were millions of things that they could focus on, yet they

Right To My Wrong

chose us.

Sawyer in particular, because she was the nice one who wouldn't say a word in defense of herself.

And she so didn't deserve their censure.

What she had happened to her was a complete and utter accident.

She'd been driving her drunk friends home when a car had pulled out in front of her.

The truck she'd been driving had pulverized the car, and with it the car's occupants.

None of the passenger's survived.

And then Sawyer had been wrongfully convicted of their murders when the father of the teen who'd been in the car falsified evidence to make it look like Sawyer was over the legal blood alcohol level.

Something she hadn't been.

After being accused, tried, and convicted, she spent eight years in Huntsville Women's Penitentiary as my cell mate, and call me selfish, but I was glad she was there.

Because if she hadn't been, I would've surely been raped every single day that I'd been in there.

But I wasn't.

And I would thank her daily for the rest of my life if I had to.

I owed her that much and more.

"What'd they say?" I asked worriedly.

Sawyer shrugged, flipping eggs onto the plate in front of her as she scooped them out of the bacon grease.

My mouth watered as she set the plate in front of me, but I crossed my arms and refused to answer once I realized she wasn't going to talk.

She sighed and leaned forward on her elbows, making sure that only I would hear what she would have to say.

"They said the same old thing. That I should still be in jail. That I killed four people, two of them promising college students. I don't know. Most of it wasn't that bad," she admitted.

I raised a brow.

"Not that bad? What do you think Silas would do if he heard what everyone was saying?" I asked.

She grimaced. "Silas wasn't there."

"Yeah, because they don't say stuff like that when he's around. Because they know he'll fight back. Which is what you should start doing. You, my manipulative friend, should have nothing but roses and fairy dust. Me, on the other hand, I've earned everything they call me. I'm a murderer. But that doesn't mean I'll let them sit there and talk badly about me while I'm right there. What they do when I'm not there is their own to deal with as they please, but by you not standing up for yourself, it means that you partially deserve it. Which you most certainly do not," I insisted.

She bit her lips between her teeth.

"I don't know how to stop them," she whispered.

The toast popped, startling us both, and I chose to keep talking while she served up Sterling's bacon and eggs.

"You tell them to stop. And if they won't, you call someone who will stop them," I told her insistently.

She shrugged. "I tried that once, and they never quit."

I crossed my arms once again and said, "Well, I'll show you how it's done when we go register you. It should be a lot of fun."

She snorted. "You're lying through your teeth about it being fun. I realize that you're doing it out of the goodness of your heart."

I winked and leaned forward, sucking half an egg into my mouth at the same moment Sterling and Loki strolled through the entrance way.

I choked, making the egg that I'd shoved into my mouth to fall to my shirt.

Completely embarrassed, I quickly wiped my shirt with the hand towel at my side, but was only effective in spreading it out all the more.

Yellow yolk sank into the porous fabric, making a very noticeable stain for all to see.

"You missed your mouth," Sterling teased as he took his seat beside me.

I flipped him off, causing him to laugh.

As well as the scary one.

"Hi, Loki. How are you?" I asked softly.

I didn't ever know what to say to the 'cops' of The Dixie Wardens.

I felt like they knew I was a bad person, and generally felt the need to stay away from me.

So I came off as a standoffish kind of person.

Not because I wouldn't like to get to know Loki, as well as the other cop, Trance, but because I was trying to protect myself.

Something some people didn't always do.

Something I hadn't always done.

But spending all those years in prison had changed me.

Had given me a certain selfishness.

Because, beside Sawyer, I had to watch out for my own back in there.

"Hello, Ruthie," Loki's deep, rumbly voice, said.

I gave him a tight smile, and he moved those piercing eyes away from me and settled them on Sawyer.

"Hey, Sawyer. How's it going, honey?" Loki asked.

See what I mean? Totally nicer to her than he was to me!

"I'm doing well, Loki. Thanks for asking. Would you like some eggs?" Sawyer asked.

I nearly choked on my cup of coffee.

Was she really going to force me to be in Loki's presence for more than just what I needed to deal with?

"Absolutely," Loki said. "Love some."

I closed my eyes and pushed my eggs around on my plate, no longer hungry at all.

It wasn't that I hated cops.

I didn't.

It's just that I felt like they hated me, which was incredibly uncomfortable.

Although, the one cop I did like, Shaw McCormick, was pretty awesome.

He was the one to get to me when I was beaten to death and I lost my little girl.

He'd held me so tenderly, cried with me hours later in my hospital room when we found out Jade wouldn't make it, and was such a good man and father that I was slightly jealous of his wife.

And still was.

Ruby Shaw was a good woman, though, and she deserved to have that man.

We were now really good friends, and had been one of the few people to stand by my side, along with Lily, when I killed my husband.

I shut off those thoughts before they got any darker.

Especially since when I looked up from my plate I could see both Loki and Sterling studying me.

"What?" I asked, directing my question at Sterling.

"I asked you what was happening with your neighbors," Loki said.

I winced.

Not only because I was ignoring Loki, either.

"Uhh," I said. "Just general problems at first. They left me notes telling me that my car was in their way and that I should park it in the driveway because it was hard to get out of their own driveway."

My driveway was full of cars that belong to the couple I'm renting from.

That'd been a stipulation of renting the house from them.

At the time, it hadn't been a big deal to me. I hadn't even had a car.

But as time had gone by, and I'd gotten a car, it started to become a bit of a hassle.

Not because of the cars in the driveway, but because of the neighbors.

I wasn't the only one who parked in the street.

Hell, the neighbor directly beside me had a fuckin' boat in front of my house, yet I didn't see any notes on *that*.

"The boat is moved," Loki nodded. "That's illegal to leave on the street. It's considered a recreational vehicle. You can park that in your yard, though. It's good he moved it or I'd have tagged it."

I blinked.

He would have?

"Technically, it's also illegal to park your car on the road over night, but it's never enforced. Mostly because it's something that everybody does. We'd have to give about half the city a ticket every night if that was the case," Loki continued. "And normally we only give out tickets like that if the car's impeding traffic. And I looked when I came in, you aren't impeding traffic."

I continued blinking.

Wow.

I didn't expect him to side with me.

"Really?" I asked. "So what was with the ticket he got off my car this morning?"

"That's my next step. But, technically, he could've felt your car was impeding traffic or something," Loki shrugged. "It's up to the discretion of the officer."

Wonderful.

Yet another thing I had to pay.

I'd have to move.

I couldn't keep living here.

Not with them calling the cops on me over something I couldn't control.

Wonderful.

Just fucking wonderful.

CHAPTER 3

Beards render birth control invalid.
-Warning to the general population

Sterling

Halligans and Handcuffs was hopping. There were so many people packed in the bar area that I was fairly sure that Ruthie was going to go insane.

I watched her move, studying her facial features to ascertain how she was doing.

She was still pissed from this morning, I could tell right off the bat.

Although she smiled and acted like her normal self, she wasn't all…there.

"Why don't you just ask her?" Loki mumbled from my side.

I turned on my barstool to look at him.

"What makes you think I'm going to ask her anything?" I asked curiously.

Normally, I was pretty good at hiding my feelings.

Had to be with a man like my father, I thought darkly.

"Probably wouldn't have noticed had I not seen you and her together at breakfast. You and her were in your own little world together that Sawyer, nor I, could see. I bet if you asked Sawyer, she'd tell you the same," Loki explained.

Hmmm. I didn't know how to feel about Loki knowing.

Because once one knew, they all knew.

But then I considered the question.

Why couldn't I ask her out?

Nothing was stopping me.

I liked her and I was fairly sure she liked me.

The only thing really standing in my way right now was my inability to pursue my dreams.

Something I'd had a problem doing since I was a young kid and my mother shattered every dream I ever had and left me to fend for myself at a fuckin' fire station.

Alone and abandoned, I'd had to make a new life.

And the new life I'd made wasn't even worth it at times.

"Uh-oh. Your girl's upset," Loki said, snapping me out of my pity party.

My eyes snapped up to focus across the room on the woman in question.

She was trying to pull her arm away from a man's grip.

And I saw red.

I don't really know how I got through the crowd of people, but in about thirty seconds flat I was at Ruthie's side and shoving the man away from her.

"Keep your hands off of her," I growled menacingly.

The man's eyes snapped with subdued fire.

"She spilled a beer on me," he growled.

"So you show your anger by putting your hands on her?" I asked in her defense.

"I'm the victim here, not her! I was just trying to push her off my junk!" the man roared.

My eyes narrowed. "Trust me, son, if she'd had her hands on your junk, you'd have known. And since I didn't hear you over here screaming in ecstasy, you obviously didn't feel the real thing yet."

I heard a few smothered laughs surrounding me, but the outraged gasp from Ruthie had me wanting to laugh.

I kept my stare on the imbecile, though.

Glaring at me, the man stood and made his way to the front door, knowing when he was no longer welcome.

"Thanks," Ruthie muttered and hustled to the kitchen without another backward glance.

Catching Loki's eye across the room, I saw him give me a slight chin lift in the kitchen's direction and sighed.

Nodding at Sebastian as I passed the bar, I walked into the kitchen to see that it was empty.

"Ruthie?" I called.

Nothing.

Eyes scanning the empty space, I finally saw the kitchen's back door ajar where it exited into the alley, and decided to follow it.

"Ruthie?" I called once again once I exited.

I could hear the sniffling before I even made it to the mouth of the alley, and my heart broke.

"What's wrong?" I asked once I spotted her hunched form.

"I'm so tired," she whispered.

I blinked, stunned.

"Why?"

"Everyone here is so freakin' mean. All I was doing was walking with a beer in my hand when somebody pushed me from behind. I swear, I don't understand what I've ever done to them. They don't know me," she said brokenly.

My heart broke.

Literally broke into a million tiny pieces for her.

I moved around her until I could see her face.

And it didn't look very good; she wasn't a pretty crier.

Her mascara was dripping down her face as the tears flowed steadily.

Her face was blotchy, and her chest was flushed red and getting redder by the second.

"Someone pushed you?" I asked for clarification.

She nodded.

"I-in the back," she said. "I didn't see anybody, though."

My face solidified to stone.

"Come on," I said, grabbing her by the hand.

"W-wait!" she cried, but I held strong to her protesting yanks and pulled her along with me.

We made it inside in time for Silas and Sebastian to make it through the kitchen door.

"I need to see the feed for the bar," I told them.

They both nodded and turned to go into the office that Silas had off the kitchen.

Silas went straight to the computer, and Sebastian went around to stand at his back.

"What part of the room?" Silas asked, looking up to stare straight at Ruthie.

Ruthie hiccupped and said, "The back quarter section."

Silas nodded and turned back to the computer, punching numbers into the computer before he said, "There."

Sebastian leaned down and pressed a few buttons, pulling it up on the TV screen directly beside us.

We watched as Ruthie passed once, twice, and then on her third pass with two glasses of beer a woman wearing a red dress got up from her chair and shoved Ruthie violently.

The rest happened as if in slow motion.

Ruthie fell forward.

The woman sat back down, laughing.

The man got his front and crotch drenched, and reflexively he sat up and clutched Ruthie by the hand.

Ruthie apologized profusely, but the man kept yelling at her.

"Who's that woman?" I snapped, watching as Silas rewound.

"I don't know," he said. "Sebastian."

Sebastian didn't need telling, he slipped from the room without another word.

"Ruthie," Silas said.

My arm wrapped around her and I pulled her into my side when she still wouldn't look up.

"Ruthie," I said softly. "You did nothing wrong."

She finally looked up at me, and as I took in her eyes filled with tears, I fell in love.

Hard and deep.

I'd known from the first time I met her months ago.

I'd just gotten home, literally just rode in from the base.

I'd pulled into the driveway of the clubhouse, surprised as hell to find that there was a welcome home party for me.

It'd been great, but the highlight of the night had been meeting Ruthie with her long strawberry blonde hair and beautiful dark gray eyes.

She had these beautiful cheery red lips that just begged to be kissed, and a pair of breasts that would fit perfectly into my hands.

The absolute best thing about her, though, was the way she acted.

I'd heard, within an hour of being there, all about Ruthie.

How she was in prison for killing her husband.

But it was how Ruthie told me within twenty minutes of knowing her that she killed her ex that made me the most happy.

She didn't hide anything.

And she told it like it was.

This sad Ruthie, however, was new.

She'd always been a fighter, ever since I'd met her.

Seeing her crying didn't make me happy.

In fact, it made me homicidal.

"Ruthie," Silas said again.

Ruthie finally looked to him.

"I fucked up," Silas said without preamble.

Ruthie's eyes widened and I smiled down at my feet.

"You heard him right," I whispered to her under my breath.

She squeezed my hand tightly as Silas continued.

"It's my job to keep my employees safe, and I didn't do that with you. I'm sorry, Ruthie. Please accept my apology," Silas told her.

Ruthie didn't say anything for a long time, I thought she wasn't going to, but obviously with the next words out of her mouth, she was just trying to collect her thoughts.

"This is my every day, Silas. I expect it...and accept it. What I don't like, though, is when it affects my tips. And lately that's been happening a lot. That woman right there," she said pointing at the screen. "Is the same that told the table next to her last week about the fact that I killed my husband. And they wrote a tip on a piece of paper saying that I should 'turn myself in.' My question to you, though, is what do you want me to do about it? I don't want to affect your business. And I feel that it is."

Silas sat back until his arms were crossed across his chest. "What makes you think that I give a fuck what everyone else thinks? This is about me and mine, not them and theirs. And you're mine...because you're Sawyer's. That's the end of it. You ever need anything, I'm here. No questions asked. Not to mention that I trust you. Honesty is important to me, and you've never given me anything but that."

Ruthie closed her eyes.

"Thank you," she whispered.

Silas stood and walked around his desk, stopping when he was a few feet in front of her.

"Don't think I don't notice how you still protect my wife. Something I've seen firsthand multiple times now. Trust me when I say that it's the least I can do," Silas rumbled.

Ruthie was clutching onto my arm, not that I thought she noticed what she was doing.

She was too busy staring into Silas' pale blue eyes.

"She got hassled at the grocery store today. Enough to scare her," Ruthie whispered.

Silas' eyes narrowed. "That woman sure doesn't know how to tell me shit when it comes to her safety."

Ruthie smiled, the first genuine one I'd seen all night.

"If she felt like your life or her child's life was in danger, she'd tell you. But if it only affects her, you'll have to pry it out of her before she tells you willingly," Ruthie informed him.

Silas winked. "That I know."

Then he stepped back and turned just as a woman was led into the room by Sebastian.

He had a grip on her arm, right below her armpit.

He wasn't having to force her, but the moment she saw Silas and Ruthie, she started to turn to leave.

"Let go of me," she ordered, pulling her arm to no avail.

She was prettier than she looked in the video feed.

Short brown hair, kissable lips. Honey brown eyes.

But behind those eyes, I could see instantly that she hated Ruthie.

Her gaze kept turning from Silas' to Ruthie's accusingly.

"You can't hold me here," the woman insisted, tugging at her arm again.

"You've got five seconds to tell me why you'd intentionally try to hurt one of my employees before I report this to the police and get you arrested. And trust me, I can pin shit on you that'll make you wish you were never such a bitch," Silas ordered her.

Ruthie's grip turned painful as her nails started to dig into the skin under my arm.

"That's the girl whose husband wanted to know all about why I was in prison. She was pissed that he was talking to me," she whispered.

Silas' eyes snapped to Ruthie's, but other than that, outwardly he didn't show that he'd even heard Ruthie's comment.

"Let's go," I said.

Ruthie clutched onto my hand gratefully.

"We're going to take off for the night, boss," I said to Silas.

Silas nodded, but didn't take his eyes off the woman in front of me.

"Tell her man to come back here as you leave," he ordered.

I winced, knowing where this was going.

Ruthie didn't ask what was going on until we'd made it to the entrance into the bar.

"What's going on?" she asked.

I held up a finger to silence her for a moment as we made it up to the table that the woman's man was sitting at, drinking a beer as if he didn't have a care in the world that his woman was being questioned in the next room.

And I knew he'd had to have seen her push Ruthie.

It happened directly in front of him.

I stopped when the table was less than a foot from me, and stared at the man until he lifted his gaze up to me.

"What?" he asked, looking me up and down.

I smiled. "Silas would like to see you in his office, please."

I said it nicely, but the man blanched.

"Knew she was going to get me in trouble when I saw her do that," he grumbled, taking his beer with him and leaving without another word.

The man was biker material if I'd ever seen it.

Long beard, bald head. Leather vest and biker boots.

Three chains hanging from his belt loop and connecting to his wallet rounded out the outfit, making him jingle as he walked directly to Silas' office without another backwards glance.

Ruthie didn't say a word as I led her out, not even to Sawyer who was trying to catch her gaze from across the room to ascertain that she was okay.

Silas most likely threatened her to get her to stay where she was, otherwise she'd have been over here trying to get all the information out of Ruthie that she could.

It also helped that she was pinned in by Torren on one side and Cleo on the other.

Two more members of The Dixie Wardens MC who were beyond loyal to Silas and the MC just like I was.

"I drove," Ruthie muttered as I started to lead her out to my bike.

I ignored her, and she didn't protest again.

Instead, she just followed me all the way to my bike, waited for me to mount and hand her my helmet, then mounted directly behind me without another word.

When she wrapped her hands around my chest, all my demons that never seemed to take a hike silenced.

I didn't think about what I had to do tomorrow.

Or what had just happened in the bar.

Not about killing people with my Glock when I saw them pop out of nowhere.

Nor did I freak out about the truck backfiring at the stop light twenty yards ahead of us.

No, with her arms around me, everything was right in my world.

Until some motherfucker in a beat up Toyota Corolla in dusty brown pulled up beside me, speeding next to me.

A flashback hit me, and I was no longer driving my bike.

I was in a beat up pickup truck in OD Green.

Parker, my right hand man and fellow BUD/S graduate was sitting beside me.

I looked over at Parker with a smile on my face, but out of my peripheral vision, I glanced a beige Corolla in my rear view mirror, speeding towards us with all the might the tiny piece of shit could muster.

In a split second decision, I decided to haul the wheel to the left just in time for the Corolla to explode.

The impact of the bomb exploding had my controlled turn bursting into a chaotic flip as the truck's wheel slipped from my hand and was wrenched free, turning so hard that the entire steering column disintegrated before my eyes.

I looked over just in time to see Parker, on fire, pulled from the truck as what was left of the Corolla smashed into the side of the truck.

Fire flashed in front of my eyes, and the last thing I heard was the screams of my good friend being burned.

"Sterling!" a woman's voice screamed in my ear.

My mind was my own again as I took stock of where I was.

I was pulled over on the side of the road, standing three feet away from my bike and staring at what I guessed was the taillights of the Corolla.

"Sterling?" the woman said again.

My gaze turned coldly to the woman on my bike, and I stared at her a long moment before I finally relaxed enough to say, "I'm sorry, Ruthie."

"Are you okay? You stopped so fast that I thought you were hurt," she asked softly.

I nodded sharply.

"That car," I rasped. "The brown one that started to creep into our lane. It caused a flashback."

She blinked, turning her head slightly to study me.

"That could've been bad," she whispered.

I nodded sharply.

"Yeah, it could have," I agreed.

"Do they happen often?" she continued.

I shook my head.

"Barely ever. It was just..." I shook my head. "About a month into my last deployment, the man I counted as one of my best friends in the world, nearly burned to death by a Corolla blowing up directly next to us. He pulled up next to us just like that one did just a few seconds ago. I can still smell the scent of his skin when it started to burn."

Bile rose in my throat, but Ruthie's words stopped the panic attack before it started.

"My husband beat me so badly that I lost our baby in the back of our Corolla," she whispered.

I blinked, turning to her sharply.

All of my problems were gone in the wake of what she'd just revealed.

"I think Corolla's are bad luck," she choked.

I made to move forward, but she held up her hand to stay my movement.

"One day I'll tell you more, but I felt that you needed something personal from me after what I just witnessed," she explained. "Just don't ask for information unless I tell you. Because it'll set off a panic attack that'll blow the socks off of your panic attack."

I laughed.

"We sound pretty fucked up."

She nodded, agreeing.

"I am. Fifty different ways, but they have two way streets and side streets, as well as under ground garages of crazy to add to the mess," she expanded.

I snorted. "Maybe one day we can compare notes. I'm not sure you could handle mine, though."

She gave me an offended look.

"I can handle just about anything. Trust me. Even alpha men like you who think they know more about what I want than I do," she shot back.

I winked at her.

"Hit a nerve?" I asked, smiling inwardly and trying my hardest not to laugh and make her think I didn't have a heart.

She shrugged. "I spent eight years trying to outtalk guards. Trust me, you're a piece of cake."

This time I really did laugh, unable to hold my façade of indifference.

"You can't handle me."

She raised a brow.

"I can't?" she challenged.

I crossed my arms and didn't flinch as the tractor trailer passed by us in a rush of air and thunder.

She, on the other hand, flinched, throwing her hand up to cover her galloping heart.

"Yeah, I can handle anything you got," she nodded.

"And how do you propose to do that?" I asked.

She shrugged. "I don't know."

"Is this something you show me while we play a round of mini golf...or laser tag?" I asked.

I was happy now.

Really happy.

This sparring we were doing was like verbal foreplay.

And I liked it.

A lot.

"I don't do mini golf," she said. "I'm more of a hot dog eating competition kind of girl. Or a monster truck rally."

"Those sound like dates...not challenges between me and you."

She smiled. "I'm sure we can find something to challenge your mind, if you need it."

I grinned. "Okay. How about two days' time? Friday at seven."

She shrugged, acting like it was no difference to her what I chose. "Okay."

"So…is this like a date?" I asked, smiling.

She patted the motorcycle seat directly in front of me.

"Dates are for teenagers," she answered.

I nodded. "And what do you call it when adults go on 'dates?'"

She grinned. "Foreplay."

CHAPTER 4

"I can't eat anymore. I'm full."
"Do you want dessert?"
"Yessssssss."
-Text from Ruthie to Sawyer

Ruthie

I got ready for our date, butterflies swirling around in my stomach like bees swarming their hive at a disturbance.

My hands were jittery.

My feet were bouncing, making the process of putting on mascara rather trying.

Once done, I smoothed my hands down my sides, surveying my appearance.

"Jewelry!" I exclaimed, almost as if I'd solved the world's hunger problem.

I closed my eyes and choked back an excited squeal as I fit my earring into my ear, finishing off the final touches of my ensemble.

I studied myself in the mirror.

I was wearing my tightest pair of jeans that I owned, which meant I probably couldn't sit down, but that was neither here nor there.

I couldn't believe I was actually going on a date with him.

It went against every ingrained protection that I'd instilled in myself.

Don't put yourself out there, and you won't get hurt.

It'd been my motto since the day I was sentenced.

I smiled at myself, leaning forward to check my teeth.

Finally happy with my appearance, I walked out of my bedroom stiffly, rethinking the whole tight pants thing.

But I decided to keep them on.

I liked the way my ass looked in them, and I assumed he would too.

That was, if he ever came.

Two hours later and there was still no Sterling.

Resigned that I waited for over two hours before I realized he wasn't coming, and when I finally did, something inside me, the only thing happy left, died.

The old Ruthann was no more.

In her place was a bitter bitch who knew she shouldn't rely on anybody.

Shouldn't have been surprised that a man like that wouldn't be interested in a woman like me.

I closed my eyes and reached my hands up to my earrings, the only ones I had left that was worth something to me.

Once they were both off, I walked to the back yard and threw them hastily in the grass.

Fuck the earrings.

Fuck my life.

Fuck everything.

I didn't care anymore.

Why bother?

Because I was only a worthless piece of shit like *he'd* always accused me of being.

The lowliest of the low.

I closed my eyes, sank down to my knees on the back porch, and cried.

***

Sterling

"Come on, come on," I growled as I called Ruthie once more.

"Shit!" I yelled, pulling my teammate's attention from their own musings to me.

"What the fuck?" Beacon, the weapon's specialist for our team, said.

"I can't get her to fuckin' answer. Do you realize what's going to happen? She's never going to give me the time of day again. Goddammit. Motherfuckin' piece of shit!" I seethed, pressing redial on my phone once again.

Once again, I got seven more rings before it went back to the generic voice message of a woman said, 'you have reached the voice mailbox of 9-0-3-7-7-7-9-7-7-4.

"Motherfucker," I growled. "Motherfucker!"

When I went to call Silas, the final sign on the plane went on indicating that all cell phone devices should be turned off, and I realized I was out of time.

Goddammit!

Seems that was my favorite word for today.

As well as all the other words.

I'd been called in less than an hour before on a mission that was 'paramount' to national security.

Seven hours before my date with Ruthie.

I'd totally forgotten about her in my haste to get my things packed and get to base.

And why it hadn't occurred to me in my six hours driving to base that I had a fuckin' date today, I didn't know, but I did forget.

And now I'd royally fucked myself.

In the ass.

With a fire poker.

A fuckin' hot one, too.

"Fuck!" I growled.

"Dude, learn a new word," another teammate, Ruben, growled.

I glared at him.

"Fuck off," I growled, roughly shoving my useless phone into my backpack and zipping it closed.

As of one hour ago, myself and my seven teammates, Parker, Ruben, Beacon, Chace, Donnie, Ellis, and Estes were all being sent to the Middle East, Iran to be specific.

The specifics of the mission hadn't been explained to us as of yet, we'd only gotten the 'get your ass on a plane' speech, and that was it.

I hadn't even realized that it wouldn't be a 'practice mission' which narrowed the amount of time it took us to get back on base and get ready until our CO was ushering us into the back of a fuckin' plane.

"Someone pissed in your cornflakes," Donnie said lightly.

I turned my glare onto him, but the man didn't flinch.

Which wasn't surprising.

He was a badass, stone cold killer.

Then again, we all were.

That was what Uncle Sam trained us to be.

"Does anybody know what we're going for?" Donnie asked, looking away from my scowl with a smile.

It wasn't Estes, our CO, who answered like I thought it would be. It was the man I'd seen in the pilot's uniform that answered the question on all of our minds.

Usually in a circumstance where we're called in like this, we know ahead of time what's on the agenda.

This time, though, we had no clue.

And I knew why moments later.

"The speaker of the house's ex-wife was visiting an army base when she was captured," the man in front of us said.

I blinked, surprised.

Why the fuck wasn't he flying the fuckin' plane?

"That's the speaker of the house," Donnie whispered at my side.

It was then I realized where I'd seen him.

On TV the night before, the one where the Speaker of The House spoke about his *pregnant* ex-wife who was missing.

He'd said that at that time, nothing was being done to bring her home, and he pleaded for her life.

And with us now on a plane to the very location she was stolen from, I assumed that something was now being done.

Must be nice to have that kind of power, I thought darkly.

It wasn't that I was objecting to saving a pregnant American's life, it was that there was no forward planning that'd taken place.

It was all thrown together too quickly, and we should've deduced a plan before we went off halfcocked.

Because that was how people got fucked up and killed, was by assholes like this who had too much power and money.

Chace was the one to ask the question that I knew everyone wanted to ask.

Chace was what I'd like to call *blunt*.

He said what was on his mind, and didn't give a shit who he offended in the process.

"And why are we going in without any knowledge of what's going on? Why rush this when this is a still hostile country? Are six lives worth it when we may get killed before we even get in there?" Chance asked.

The man, Jason Reid, turned towards Chace and narrowed his eyes.

"What your job is, Marine, is to follow orders," Reid growled.

Chace narrowed his eyes and stood, moving closer to the man.

Estes stopped him before he could get up in his face.

"I'm a fucking SEAL, not a goddamn Marine. And maybe you should get that straight before you send us in somewhere where we won't come back out alive…unless that's not your main priority here," Chace hissed.

I looked around the belly of the transport plane we were currently flying in, and wondered if it could withstand hurricane Chace. I decided that it should hold up to him if we were able to take Chace's rifle away from him.

Silence continued, so long that you could practically cut the testosterone filled air around us with a fuckin' knife.

"All you guys have to do is find my ex-wife, get her out, and we'll get home. She's in a hotel with a man named Yamir Drakmar. She was taken the moment she got off the plane. He's got no men in the hotel and, as far as we can tell, she was meant to meet him there. However, my ex-wife sent me a picture of the man the moment she touched down just to be safe, and I had my closest advisor run the picture through facial recognition software. And he's wanted in over fifteen countries, and is on our America's Most Wanted List for a bomb threat at the Seattle Airport in November of 2007."

I should've known that this mission wouldn't be like all the rest.

Should've known that it wouldn't be that easy.

Should've known that we'd all die.

CHAPTER 5

Don't hate me because I'm beard-iful.
-Bumper Sticker

Ruthie

Three weeks later

SEAL Team eleven has been missing for three weeks now with no bodies or demands from Iran. From what we've been able to tell, the negotiation for The Speaker of the House's ex-wife, Darynda Reid, was not successful.

I closed my eyes as I listened to the word of SEAL Team eleven from the reporter on CNN's mouth.

How I knew that that was Sterling's team, I didn't know.

I didn't have any confirmation.

It was only a hunch.

Because after I got over my pity party, I knew that he wouldn't have left unless he absolutely *had* to.

I also knew, by way of Sawyer asking her husband, that Sterling hadn't been seen at the club, either.

And he wouldn't have just left Cormac and Garrison, nor the club.

Which meant he didn't leave me.

But I wasn't happy about hearing that, because it meant I was hearing what I was hearing from the stupid blonde reporter's mouth, and seeing a fiery wreckage where some fleabag motel *used* to be.

No names have been released by the Pentagon as of yet, but we expect it to be only a matter of time before the president holds a press conference releasing the information on the eight man team.

"Oh, no," I moaned. "Oh *no*."

It was later that night that I stupidly sent the text message.

It was short and sweet, but it relayed every bit of emotion I felt.

Ruthie: You owe me a date, or was what you said all for show?

There was no reply.

***

Three weeks later

The Pentagon still refuses to give out the names of SEAL team eleven. They're still convinced of the safety of this team, even though all evidence shows to the contrary.

I'd been torturing myself by watching CNN for going on six weeks now.

When I wasn't working at the bar, the news was on.

Dane absolutely hated watching the news, but when I reacted rather flamboyantly when he tried to change it the first time I watched it at work, he stopped complaining or trying.

I couldn't really tell you why I was watching the news.

Most of the time they didn't even cover SEAL Team Eleven's disappearance.

As the weeks had passed, slowly the new news started to cover up the old.

Now they were playing the same story of a man who'd tried to kill his wife, over and over again.

They were dissecting his motives, as well as his past life.

At night, though, when my favorite reporter came on, was when I got the real information.

It seemed that the show's host and reporter, Gordon Matthews, cared about his country and those that protected it.

He of course touched on the other hot topics, but the majority of his time was spent on what was happening with our troops on the other side of the world.

Gordon, what do you think is the White House's reasoning behind their refusal to give any names out? A woman on the screen asked him.

I froze in the kitchen of Halligans and Handcuffs, where I sometimes snuck breaks so I could see if anything new had transpired over my shifts, and stared at the flat screen hanging on the wall.

Being a Navy SEAL is a tremendous accomplishment. However, they put a lot of time and effort into becoming a SEAL, and maintaining their status as a SEAL. Their identity is their protection. They rely on their identities being secret while they're over there. What if they're alive, and their pictures are splashed all over every TV screen in the world? If they're taking cover waiting for the fire to die down, and see their face on the TV screen, how are they supposed to protect themselves? They'll be sitting ducks in a country that still doesn't trust us, and no one to protect them or have their backs. Trust me when I say what they're doing is protecting themselves as well as the soldiers that protect this country by not giving out names.

I smiled at the screen.

That'd been about what I was thinking, and he'd said it eloquently.

"He's okay," Silas' deep voice rumbled from my side.

I whipped around; heart pounding a million miles an hour.

"How do you know?" I gasped.

He winked. "That boy has street smarts that you wouldn't believe. Met him when he was eighteen and a thief who thought I was trying to steal his dinner. Trust me when I say that he's alive. They wouldn't be stalling for time if they didn't think the same."

I went back to work, but Silas' words stayed in the front of my mind.

He just had to be okay.

I'd never worried about anyone this much unless they meant something to me.

And I was afraid to admit it, but the longer it went that he was gone, the more I realized how attached I'd become to him.

***

Three weeks later

I bit my fingernails down to the cuticle.

Again.

Here I was, on a Saturday night, biting my fingernails and eating a gallon of ice cream while I stayed glued to the news.

SEAL Team Eleven believed alive.

An eight member team of some sort is seen here leaving the Saudi Arabian embassy. None of their identities can be confirmed, but it is believed that this is the team that went missing two months ago, after a botched mission gone wrong. Nothing has been proven yet, but Fox News will visit this new development upon the hour.

Was that him?

They looked a lot smaller than what I thought Sterling should look, but if he was in hiding for nine weeks, then that only made sense.

My phone pinged at my side, and before looking at it, I scooped a humongous wedge of ice cream onto my spoon that was made for two mouths instead of one, and pulled it up to my face to read the message.

Kraken: It wasn't all for show. Come outside.

My brows furrowed.

Kraken?

What the fuck, and who the hell was that?

I'd never programmed a 'Kraken' into my phone.

But, like the dumb movie heroine who always gets killed in the scary movies, I walked outside with my large spoon in my hand, still holding my ice cream.

Thinking I was being smart, I unlocked the back door and slowly slipped into the night.

It was raining.

Like it always was here.

It felt like I'd moved to Seattle with all the rain we'd been getting.

Luckily, the house was equipped with a wraparound porch, even if it did need fixing in places.

I knew where to avoid, though.

And apparently so did the man that snuck up behind me and pulled me into a warm, hard, *extremely hard*, body.

A metal clang announced the melting spoon of ice cream hitting the ground at the surprise.

"Trying to sneak up on me?" The man asked.

My heart was pounding, but not because I was scared. Not anymore.

Because I was over the fucking moon!

"Sterling!" I cried, wiggling in his arms until I had my arms around his neck.

He let me, of course, but I didn't notice as I hugged him tight.

"You're okay!" I cried.

"Mmmmhmm," he hummed. "A-Okay."

I leaned back until my hands were pressed on either side of his face, fingers grazing his beard that'd grown exponentially since I'd last seen him.

His hair had as well, from what I could tell by my emergency lights that'd flicked on the moment I'd passed.

I'd ask him later how he'd managed *not* to set them off.

"You missed our date!" Was the next thing I could think to say.

He smiled. "Yeah, I did. I'll have to make that up to you."

His rumbled reply was felt deep inside of me as I started to take note at how close our bodies were.

His arms circled me, holding me off the floor with hilarious ease.

One arm was under my ass, and the other was banded across my lower back.

My crotch was pressed to his hard belly, and I could feel the distinct outline of what I guessed to be his cock, or possibly a baton of some sort, *which I sincerely doubted*, pressing against my thighs.

And yes, I do mean *thighs*.

It started at the edge of one and traveled across the length of the other, making me swallow hard.

"H-how are you going to make it up to me?" I rasped, licking my lips.

He grinned, and suddenly the security light blinked out, plunging us into darkness once again.

The thunder and rain boomed all around us, surrounding us in a blanket that consisted of only him and me, our breathing, and my body pressed against his.

He moved quickly, pinning me so that I had my back pressed up against the siding of my house.

I gasped, instinctually opening my legs to allow him to move in between them.

He took the invitation, pressing further into me, and proving once and for all that what I'd previously called a baton was indeed a part of him.

A very hard, very warm, yummy part of him.

"What..." I licked my lips and tried again. "What are you doing?"

He pressed more weight onto me, hitching me up higher so I wasn't against his happy place anymore. "I don't know."

His head fell forward until it was resting on my collarbone, and I knew then that he really didn't know.

And he wasn't okay.

I placed my hand on both of his shoulders, moving them up over the column of his neck until they came to a rest on his cheeks.

"Sterling?" I asked.

He tilted his head back, and the movement somehow flipped the switch for the motion detected flood light once again.

It turned on, and the light displayed actual pain on Sterling's face.

"Are you okay?" I whispered.

"I shouldn't be here," he grimaced and started to let me go, but I knew if he let me go, he'd leave.

And I *really* didn't want him to leave.

I was happy that he'd come.

Happy that I was one of the first places he came once he'd gotten back home.

I wrapped my arms around his neck, sank my mouth down to his, and planted a kiss on his lips.

The move made him still, and then suddenly I was being divested of my pants.

Roughly.

"Sterling," I gasped, but I didn't make him stop.

It wasn't a gasp of disapproval, but a sincere gasp of surprise at the movement.

And in no way, shape, or form was it a denial of what I knew he was about to do.

And I'd never wanted anything more in my life.

His hard cock was suddenly at my entrance, and he slowly sank inside of me, one delicious inch at a time until I could barely gather breath to fill my lungs.

I couldn't tell you whether it was due to the fact that he was big, or the fact that I was just that rusty at sex, but I felt like he was splitting me in two.

He didn't even let me complain, only started to fuck me with hard, powerful strokes.

It started out as slightly painful, but the desperation in his thrusts, as well as the need inside me, paired with the overall excitement that he was here, alive, and in my arms made me a slow burn start to build in my core.

I knew we should be wearing a condom.

Which was okay, I guess, in a sense.

I was on the pill. We just hadn't had the discussion about it yet.

But I knew he was healthy as I was.

I also knew that if he'd pulled out right then, that I might have become physically violent.

Lucky for him he didn't stop, only revved up even more when he felt my pussy start to pulse around him, signaling my impending release.

"Sterling," I moaned loudly. "Oh, my…fuck…oh, God!"

His mouth went to the exposed column of my throat, and he sucked.

Hard.

I hadn't ever had a hickey before, but I knew I would this time.

And I didn't care.

At all.

Sterling shifted his hips, and reached down until both of his arms were holding my legs up.

His hands planted onto the wall behind me, and suddenly the only thing touching me was his hard arms behind my knees, and his cock splitting me.

And as I looked down, the security light only highlighting bits and pieces of our bodies as they moved as one, I came.

My world shattered with a loud boom that had the very air around us shaking,

Logically I knew it was thunder, but at that moment in time, I couldn't give less of a fuck.

My mind was so focused on this…on him…that I couldn't separate the two things.

He watched me come, and my eyes stayed ensnared by his.

"Sterling," I gasped his name, and he finally let go.

He came hard inside my tightened pussy, shooting himself down so deep inside me that I knew I'd be feeling him there for days.

Both of us panted in the revamped storm, cold rain pounded my bare legs where Sterling held them in place, which meant his ass was surely getting wet since I could now see that his pants were down around his ankles.

A flash of lightening had the world lighting up around us, and I saw the need, as well as the pain, still deep in his eyes.

"You wanna come inside?" I asked him softly.

He nodded, but didn't say anything, only dropping my knees one by one until I rested on tippy toes.

His cock was still buried deep inside of me, and hadn't gone down one single bit since he'd come.

In fact, he was still pulsing hard inside of me with the beat of his heart.

The new position, with my legs down, let his hard cock rest deliciously against my clit, and each beat of his heart, pulse of his dick, had me nearly clenching in anticipation.

"I need you again," he whispered roughly.

I nodded. "Okay."

This time was slower.

Much slower.

He pulled out and bent me forward on my porch railing.

I had an irrational thought of being excited that we were doing it in such a public place.

But, realistically, I knew that no one could see us.

Not with the way the rain was pouring down.

The wind blew, spraying me with a light mist across my face just as Sterling sank back inside of me.

I moaned and threw my head back, eyes closing again as he started to slowly push into me, before starting the long pull back out.

I clutched onto the wooden railing with tight fists, holding on for dear life as he gave me all he had to give.

I don't know how long that went on.

Minutes. Hours. Hell, I didn't know and I didn't really care.

All I knew right then was that he was with me, and I was with him.

And when I came long minutes later, pulling him with me along the way, I had never felt anything so right.

***

"I heard something disturbing today while Silas and Sawyer were talking. And I wanted to make sure that I spoke with you about it to make sure I wasn't going to flip any triggers for you. Although I'd intended to talk to you about it before I…*you know*…you," Sterling said later that night.

My head was pillowed on his chest, and his fingers were sifting through my hair.

"How long have you been home?" I asked softly.

He answered instantly.

"Last night around eleven P.M.," he answered. "But nobody's seen me yet. I only went to Silas' place to grab my spare key. Mine was…lost. Which was where I heard them talking about the things that happened to you while you were in prison."

He twirled my hair around his finger, playing with it and making me nearly purr.

I loved having my hair played with.

We'd just finished round three of the best sex I'd ever had in my life, and I was fairly positive that my legs wouldn't be holding me up any time soon.

"I was never raped, even though Sawyer thinks otherwise," I told him on a sigh. "Although they thought I had some questionable diseases. I was taken away and made to look like I was raped to scare the other women. I never told anybody any differently. Maybe I should have…but it kept me safe. Kept Sawyer safe."

I could hear his mind racing, wondering if I actually had any 'questionable diseases' or not.

"I don't have any," I said instantly. "They checked that almost monthly, and I had my own tests the moment I escaped that place. And I haven't had sex with anyone in well over ten years."

"That's good to know, honey. Although it wasn't the question on my mind," he rumbled.

His chest rattled with each word he spoke, and my free hand that wasn't supporting my head started to run through the hair on his chest, teasing its way down to tangle in the hair surrounding his groin.

"Then what was?" I asked softly.

His penis started to stir when my hands played with the hair, but he didn't act on it, leaving me to play with him as he spoke.

"The question on my mind was whether they'd even tried. And how many times they tried before you had to make up a god awful lie like that to keep from being raped," he mumbled.

I winced.

My mind had automatically gone to the worst possible scenario he could be thinking. I should've known he'd never think badly about me.

"They tried. The men guards think we've been put in the cage for their pleasure…at least with some of them. They tried with Sawyer as well, but the two of us stuck together. Found a way to make it work. I can't say it was a fun eight years in there, but it was definitely bearable," I told him. "It could've been way worse."

He didn't say anything to that.

And I imagined he wasn't very happy with that admission.

"If they weren't all in jail, I'd kill them," he said roughly.

I knew he would, too.

Sterling was the 'protector.'

He wanted to make sure everyone was taken care of before himself.

Something that I'd witnessed quite a few times since I'd been released from prison.

"They're in jail…and Silas did kill the one that was the main problem," I shuddered.

I'd seen pictures, because I'd asked Silas to show them to me.

I wanted to know that he was dead.

I was tired of living my life scared.

My entire existence was spent wondering.

Would I be able to eat today?

Would I ever find a home to live in?

Would I graduate college?

Would I be alive when I saw twenty-two?

Would Bender hurt our child?

How would I get away from him if he did hurt us?

Then I'd gone to jail, accused of killing my husband; not for my protection, but for vengeance.

And it'd sucked.

And the questions started anew.

Only they kept getting worse and worse.

Then I got out…and I met Silas…and Sterling.

And I realized that maybe, just maybe, life wasn't so bad.

Then Sterling disappeared, and I was left thinking about a man that I didn't have any attachment to, other than a few emotional strings.

Strings that held captive as I waited nine weeks for him to get home…to hear word that he was even alive.

And he was finally here.

"What happened over there?" I asked softly.

He shook his head. "I can't really talk about it."

"Can you tell me anything?" I asked.

"A little bit," he answered, sitting up until his back was against my headboard.

My hand that'd been playing with his belly hair fell free from him, and he pulled the sheet up until it was resting lightly over both legs, covering the goods.

His eyes stared blankly forward as he said, "You know I'm an active member of SEAL Team Eleven, right?"

I nodded. "I assumed."

"Yeah, the whole country will know about the SEAL team now that we're home. But we were called to perform a mission that wasn't well thought out in the least, and we nearly died because of it," he explained.

"Did your whole team survive?" I asked.

He nodded.

"Yeah, not with any help from Uncle Sam, though. We had to do it all on our own, cross into two countries before we were able to get out safely," he answered.

"Wow," I whispered. "Did you get hurt?"

I knew he was hurt.

I could tell because he couldn't quite hide the winces each time I pressed too hard on his right shoulder.

I'd yet to see his back, but I knew he had some type of…something…there.

I felt something on the back of his right shoulder, but the moment I started to turn to look at it, he'd distracted me with round three.

It'd been a rather thorough distraction, too.

Now, though, I wouldn't be so easily deterred.

"So what now?" I asked softly, sitting up until I was crossed legged in the bed.

He shook his head. "Keep working. One bad mission won't stop us. The only one that will stop us will be the ones that kill us."

I tried not to let that sink in too deep.

The thought of him being killed, while on a mission, scared the crap out of me.

Not that I had any right to demand he be careful, it slipped out of my mouth nonetheless.

"You need to be careful, Sterling. You have a lot of people that would miss you if you were gone. Silas didn't actually express being worried, but he always had the news on every time I saw him," I whispered, picking at the invisible lint on the sheet.

"What about you?" He asked.

I blinked, looking up at him. "What about me?"

He smiled, his beautiful eyes full of mirth now instead of pain.

"Will you miss me?" He asked.

"*Would* I miss you? Yes. *Will* I miss you? No, because you're not going anywhere," I answered.

He grinned, and I realized he was happy with that answer.

Really happy.

"So about that date…"

I shook my head. "I need to go to sleep. I have to work in the morning."

He moved quickly.

One second I was staring at his throat, admiring his jaw and mouth, and the next he was pinning me to the bed, his hard cock pressing into my exposed sex.

Only the sheet was between us, and it wasn't much of a barrier for the beast he had between his legs.

"Call in sick," he said, his mouth only a whisper away from my own.

I shook my head. "I can't. I'm opening tomorrow."

He looked at the clock at my bedside, and then back to me.

"What time do you have to be there?" He countered.

I looked at the clock myself and winced.

"In about two hours," I answered.

His brows rose.

"And what exactly do you do when you get there that early?" He asked.

"I open…" I trailed off.

He tickled me and I squealed.

"Stop! Ack!" I screamed and laughed.

"What I meant," he said, removing his fingers. "Was what do you do once you get there? Are you busy?"

I shook my head. "No. Why?"

"You up for some company?" He wondered.

I nodded. "Yeah, I could do some company."

He laughed. "You already 'did' the company. More than once."

I reached forward and grasped his nipple between two fingers and twisted slightly.

He shot off me like a rocket, laughing the whole way.

"Let's go get breakfast. And have that date," he answered, pulling up his pants that I hadn't seen him step into.

I blinked.

"Me going to work doesn't count as a date," I told him.

He smiled.

"Yeah, but I just gotta make sure you don't get lost when our date finally does happen. So, I'll be sticking close," he informed me, picking up my pants I'd had on outside when he'd texted me.

Which reminded me.

"Why are you programmed as Kraken in my phone?" I asked.

He grinned. "I came in last night for my key and snuck your phone from behind the bar. Reprogrammed myself. That's my club name."

I blinked.

"How did you do that with nobody seeing you?" I asked incredulously.

He pointed at himself, declaring, "SEAL baby. It means I can do things most normal people can't."

"Full of yourself much?" I asked, dropping the pants in favor of a pair of blue jeans at the foot of my bed.

"The only one who's 'full of me' is going to be you if you don't get dressed in the next fifteen seconds," he shot back.

I hastily pulled on my jeans, smiling at him over my shoulder.

"Got it."

CHAPTER 6

*Sometimes I want to rub Sterling's beard like my lucky rabbit's
foot.
-Ruthie's secret thoughts*

Sterling

"This isn't safe at all," I muttered to myself as I took in the darkened gas station.

I'd seen it in passing at night, but never really correlated it with Ruthie being here working.

There wasn't a single light on in the parking lot, and once you turned the light on inside, you were highlighted perfectly while you couldn't make out a single goddamn thing outside.

And my SEAL training was screaming at me to get the fuck out of such a high profile spot.

"Would you chill out? You're scaring away the customers," Ruthie admonished as she started flicking on all of the coffee makers.

I looked back at the parking lot that had yet to see a single customer.

"There haven't been any here at all. How would I have scared them away?" I asked, confused.

Ruthie tossed a smile over her shoulder. "I was teasing. Something that obviously went right over your head. Hey, will you do me a favor and bring me a bucket of ice out of the back?"

She pointed in the direction of a doorway, one I remembered looking into earlier when we'd first arrived.

All that was in it was an ice machine and some extra supplies such as coffee cups, napkins, and straws.

I went and did what she asked, hearing the door jingle not even thirty seconds after I started filling up the bucket.

I came out with my hand grasped around the metal handle to see Ruthie flirting away with an older man that looked to be in his mid-nineties.

Was he even able to drive a car anymore? He could barely walk.

But he could talk.

"Ruthie, you didn't get me a cup yet, did'ja darlin'?" The old man asked.

Ruthie smiled at him. "No, Mr. Adams. I just got here myself. My man decided to make me late."

I felt my chest expand as she called me her 'man.'

I'd never really had anyone in my life call me their own and it felt really good to hear someone be possessive of me.

"Oh, did he get cheeky with you to make you late?" Mr. Adams asked teasingly, walking stiffly over to the metal counter where all the drinks were being held.

He pulled the half done coffee pot out of its holder and held his shaking hand underneath the flow of coffee still pouring out of the pot.

Once he had it filled, he replaced the pot with surprising agility and placed the paper cup onto the counter where he proceeded to fill it up with so much sugar that I was fairly sure it could be nothing but sludge at the bottom.

"He just complains a lot about my safety," Ruthie said, turning a wink on me before she went over to Mr. Adams and put a lid on his coffee cup. "Seems SEALS are overly cautious."

It was almost as if she'd done it so many times that it was a sort of routine for them.

"Being safe isn't a bad thing. When I was in the war, I came home doing a lot of things differently. Like I used to check my locks five times a night. God forbid I hear a creak I couldn't explain, which meant I was doing the lock thing again. My guns were always at the ready, too. My wife, bless her sweet heart, hated it. But she loved me and lived with it, which is what I assume you're doing by that smile on your face," Mr. Adams said.

Her eyes locked with mine, startled.

I couldn't say that it was fear in her eyes, per se, but it was something.

Hope? Nervousness?

Maybe them all.

I didn't know.

What I did know was that what I felt for Ruthie went beyond just the physical.

While I'd been pinned down in Iran, I'd had a lot of time do some much needed thinking.

Thinking about my life.

How I wanted things to go for me. Who I wanted in my life. What I wanted to do for the rest of it.

But I had to survive first.

And there were times in the last nine weeks where I wasn't sure I was going to.

But Ruthie had been at the front of my mind through it all. It'd been her face I'd seen when I'd nearly lost my life when I was hightailing it out of a dark alley, a barrage of gunfire following the team out.

We'd been ambushed.

Soldiers were at the ready the moment we'd stepped foot onto the street at that flea bitten motel.

We'd never even seen the pregnant ex-wife, nor the man who'd brought her to that cesspool sandbox of a country.

"You gonna bring that ice over here or do I need to do it myself, son?"

My eyes snapped back from where the blank stare I'd been giving the sign above the coke machine.

"Yeah, I'll get it," I said, bringing the bucket to the machine and pouring it hole high at the top where Ruthie indicated.

"It's more fun to watch her climb up on the ladder and do that herself," Mr. Adams said.

I tossed him a grin.

"She does have a fine ass," I agreed.

Ruthie gasped.

He winked, but his face smoothed to somber as he turned to Ruthie.

"I say, you should really control this man," Mr. Adams said as he started shuffling to the front door. "I'll pay you tomorrow. I forgot my wallet in the truck, and it'd take me longer to go out there and get it than I want. I don't move like I once did. And the fish are gonna be biting soon if I don't hurry."

With that he slipped out into the still predawn air, leaving the jingling of the door in his wake.

"He was nice," I said, taking the bucket back into the storage room.

"Will you grab me a box of straws off the top shelf?" She yelled.

I grabbed the box and started back outside, but stilled when I saw the man coming into the store.

He looked shady as fuck.

Long shaggy hair. Wild eyes.

Dirty grunge covered jeans, tennis shoes that looked like they should've been retired long ago. And the shirt was so covered in filth that I wanted to cringe.

When was the last time the man took a bath?

Or washed his clothes?

Not waiting to see what he wanted, I walked back out, placing the box on the counter next to Ruthie who still had her back to the customer as she straightened up the straws and cups in the dispenser in front of her.

"Can I help you?" I asked.

He jerked, surprised that I'd actually spoken to him.

"Yeah," he said licking his lips. "You got a dollar you can spare?"

I reached into my back pocket, withdrew my wallet, and fished a dollar out of it and folded it in two before handing it to him.

Although I knew what he was going to do before I even saw him move, I still gave him the benefit of the doubt.

He reached forward and tried to snatch the entire wallet out of my hand, but I snapped my arm back and placed myself in front of Ruthie before aiming the gun that suddenly appeared in my hand pointed at the man's face.

He froze.

"Don't," he whispered.

"Give me a reason," I growled.

Ruthie slowly turned, but stayed plastered to my back, not even peeking her head over my shoulder to get a look.

Good girl.

I could feel her softness sinking into me, and I hated that she was there right then.

What would've happened had I not been there?

"I need it, man. I just need it," he chattered, arm rising to scratch at his neck viciously.

I shook my head. "Go to the hospital. Get yourself cleaned up."

He shook his head. "I can't. They said I had to bring them money or they'd kill her."

"Her who?" I asked sharply, startling the man.

"My dog," he explained like it was completely rational that whoever it was would threaten his dog if he didn't pay the money he owed.

And genuinely it would've worked with some people.

I wasn't some people, though.

I was me.

I couldn't say I'd been in his exact same position before, but I knew what desperation felt like.

Yet here I was, making something of myself.

The man standing in front of me probably had some of the same possibilities that I had, yet he'd chosen a different path in life.

"Get out of here," I barked, holstering my gun.

He ran, not looking back, and I felt Ruthie finally settle at my back.

"Shit," she whispered. "He's never done that before."

I blinked and moved until I could look out the doors.

It was finally lightening up outside, which meant I could see that the man had run.

He was no longer in the parking lot, but what she'd just said didn't make my heart rate decrease any.

"He's never done that before?" I asked for clarification.

She shook her head. "Normally, I just give him the dollar and he leaves."

I gritted my teeth and walked closer to her. "Does your boss know this man?"

She shrugged. "I don't know. He's the one who opens when I'm not, so I only assume he does."

"And the sight of that man never raised any red flags with you?" I asked.

She shook her head. "He's just down on his luck."

"Really down on his luck," I muttered to myself, pulling my phone out of my pocket.

"What are you doing?" She asked in surprise.

"Calling the police. They need to know what happened, that way if it ever happens again a report is on file for it," I told her.

She rolled her eyes. "I already said he's harmless."

"I don't care if he's 'harmless' as you say he is. Just make sure you always keep your distance from him, and stop being so trusting. Everyone has a past, and I saw the violence in his eyes. He was desperate today, what do you think will happen if three days pass and he still doesn't have what he wants?" I asked her.

She pursed her lips. "I don't know."

I studied her face for a long moment before I said, "He'll come back. He knows you'll give him money, next time he'll be smarter about who he comes in here with, too."

She nodded. "I'll be careful. Dane said something about allowing us to carry a shotgun under the counter. Maybe it'd be a good thing to start that."

I gave her a raised brow. "Do you know how to shoot a shotgun?"

She shook her head. "No. But don't you just point and shoot?"

I shook my head.

I mean really, was the owner just going to say, 'Here's a gun. Shoot anyone that you feel needs to be shot?'

"Before you tell him that, I'll take you out to the range and teach you. When do you open next?" I asked.

She closed her eyes and tilted her head slightly. "I'm not allowed to own a gun."

I stopped to think about that for a moment.

Of course she wouldn't be able to.

"Are...do you mind telling me...how you killed him?" I asked, leaning my ass against the counter.

It'd been weighing on my mind.

Not the fact that she'd killed him, but the fact that she'd *had* to kill him.

What had happened that she needed to resort to those kinds of measures?

All I'd been able to gather from Silas was that she'd been abused and scared for her life.

I had no details on the rest.

She looked down at her hands where they were buried in the box full of straws, and closed her eyes like she'd just gotten done with an intense workout.

The one where you see the couch after a long day at work of doing nothing but standing on your feet, and you know you're about to get some comfort.

This sigh Ruthie let out was no different.

"I met Bender when I was in college. He had gone to the same high school as Lily and I and we had unknowingly followed him to Louisiana. I hadn't ever really noticed him until college, though. I had a crush on him from the moment I saw him, but his eyes were all for Lily, my best friend," she told me. "But when he saw that Lily had the hots for Dante, his best friend, he slept with me to try to make her jealous. Me, being the naïve girl that I was, had no clue that'd been why he'd done it. I was only happy to be noticed. So we got together that night, and weeks later with nothing from him, I found out I was pregnant."

She smashed the straws into the holder and turned around, thrusting her fingers into her hair.

"I told him what happened, and he acted like I was a piece of lint to be picked off his shirt. Gave me a '*that sucks*' and went on about his business. But my pregnancy had been difficult, and bills started piling up." She shook her head. "I don't really know how it happened, but his parents somehow found out, and forced him to marry me. Something else I didn't know at the time." Her head hung. "I was so happy not to be alone through that, that I jumped at the chance."

She started, lurched forward and folded the box closed, needing something to do with her hands as she said, "We married, but he was abusive. Resented everything about me that he could. At first it was all just verbal attacks, but they slowly morphed into physical attacks when I was five months pregnant. It was bad. He was six foot five inches and over three hundred pounds. Was a star athlete at ULM. Played in three sports. And he was so muscular." She rested both hands on the top of the box, and I finally couldn't take it anymore.

I moved forward and gathered her into my arms.

"Yeah?" I asked.

She felt tiny in my arms.

I wasn't that big, only six foot three, and two hundred and thirty pounds, but the sound of the man she'd once been wed to sounded massive.

He'd dwarf her five foot two inch frame.

And imagining hitting this woman with any force whatsoever made rage pour into my gut.

My mind drifted back to memories of my mother with each man she used to pick up on any given day.

Though a few of them weren't what I would call 'abusive,' the vast majority of them were.

Seriously.

Although if there was one thing I could say about my mother, she always protected me.

Even when she gave me up for adoption at thirteen, she was protecting me.

Which had made the entire thing hurt even worse, knowing that she hadn't wanted to give me up.

But she'd fallen in with a bad crowd, and couldn't see a way out.

So she'd had a friend drop me off at a fire station.

I'd been coached for hours on what to say and not to say to the authorities.

It helped that I looked a lot younger than I actually was.

So I was put into the foster system, and haven't seen my mother since that day fourteen years before.

Not that I hadn't tried to look for her.

I'd looked a lot.

It was just that wherever she was at, she had protection now.

The little bit I'd gathered on her whereabouts all pointed to protection and *not* danger.

So I'd let her be, even though it broke my heart to do so.

"When I was around eight months pregnant, Bender beat me so badly that I couldn't *not* go to the hospital. I had to make sure my baby was all right. And when I got there, they told me that my baby had suffered multiple traumas and was no longer alive," she choked.

I snapped back out of my own head with a jarring yank, and I was just as mad now as I'd been earlier.

Child abuse was a hard limit for me.

I'd grown up protected from it until I'd gotten into the foster home with Cormac and Garrison, and there our supposed 'foster parents' took turns beating the shit out of us if we didn't get our housework done on time.

Something that happened quite often seeing as they expected so much of us.

But right then, my focus was all on Ruthie and the tears that she was crying into my shirt.

"I pressed charges on him. For the first time in seven months, I finally pressed charges…when it no longer counted," she whispered brokenly.

Her sobs were tearing through my armor that I used to surround my heart.

To hold me back from this very sort of thing.

If you felt, you hurt.

There was no way around it.

If you cared, and trust me, it was something that I tried valiantly not to do, you *always* end up hurt.

"You weren't too late," I told her. "And the charges did count."

She shook her head.

"He was arrested, and in jail for only an hour. An hour, Sterling," she rasped. "And I knew, the moment he came up on the man that was changing our locks that he wasn't going to stop. He didn't care. He felt like I was the reason for his bad luck. That I was the reason he didn't get Lily like he wanted."

I held her tighter, knowing where this was going before the words even left her lips.

"He slapped me in passing, knocking me down and then went into the bathroom. So I went into the bedroom that we shared. Where I slept next to him night after night, scared as hell but knowing he'd accept nothing less from me, and picked up the gun he liked to wave in my face when he was feeling particularly feisty," she choked. "And the moment he started to pee, I shot him. In the heart. Because I knew if I didn't, he'd kill me."

I ran my beard along her face, trying to help the emotions I knew were barreling away inside her.

"I don't think I would have done a damn thing differently," I whispered. "Not a single damn thing."

Hell, I was in an abusive situation for eighteen years of my life.

I got away from it the moment I could safely do so.

I could've told somebody.

But I didn't.

Why?

I couldn't really tell you.

When you're in a situation like that, you don't see things the same as you do once you're free and clear of it.

You see them with these glasses on.

It's like you're aware that what's going on is bad, but you don't think you can get away.

And in Ruthie's situation, she knew that once she reported what was going on to the authorities, something would happen to her.

So she'd taken precautions.

Not everyone reaches that point.

I never reached that point.

But Ruthie lost something that I'd never had.

A child that she'd loved with all of her heart.

And who wouldn't react the way Ruthie had?

"What are you doing to my employee?" A man barked.

I looked up to see the owner of the place there, staring at Ruthie in horror looking like he was about to do violence against me on her behalf.

"Dane, this is Sterling. You know him," she said in exasperation.

Dane's eyes narrowed.

"Is this the boy that you kept making me watch the news for?" He grumbled crossing his beefy arms over his chest.

She nodded, biting her lip and glaring quickly at me before turning back to Dane.

"Yeah, this is him. He's okay, though," she told Dane.

"I can see that. Very healthy…" he said, looking pointedly at my crotch.

I laughed.

Ruthie, however, missed the whole interaction.

"So I'm guessing you want the day off," he grumbled, starting forward.

Ruthie shook her head. "Not really, no. I was just hoping you wouldn't mind that he's here with me. I need the money."

"You have vacation, you know," Dane informed her, taking a seat on the stool behind the counter.

Ruthie nodded. "Yeah, but I'm saving that up for something important."

His brows rose. "What you got to do that's important that you need a whole fourteen days for?"

She pursed her lips. "I don't know. But something might come up."

I could figure out something to do with fourteen days.

And it involved lots and lots of cardio.

"Take your man and get out of here. Have breakfast. Be here tomorrow at nine. I got you for today," he said, standing up and offering his hand to me. "Glad you made it home, son. You would've had one upset girl on your hands had anything bad happened to you."

I looked down at Ruthie's averted eyes, and realized that I did, in fact, have something good on my hands.

Something I planned to take care of indefinitely.

Whether she wanted me to or not.

CHAPTER 7

There's a chance this is vodka.
-Coffee Cup

Sterling

I walked into the bar of Halligans and Handcuffs, Ruthie's hand in mine, and came to a sudden halt directly inside the door.

"What?" I asked the men standing there like they'd seen a ghost.

Kettle, Silas, Torren, Loki, Trance, Sebastian, and Dixie were all standing there by the bar, frozen to the spot and staring at me.

Then, my brothers surrounded me.

The men I counted as men of my blood even when they weren't.

The men who were genuinely happy that I was back.

Which made me feel bad.

I should've told them I was okay three days ago.

But I'd only thought about getting home. Then I'd only thought about Ruthie's hot voodoo pussy.

"Shit, Kraken," Dixie exclaimed. "Where the fuck have you been?"

I smiled as nonchalantly as I could, hoping beyond hope that he didn't read in my eyes how bad it'd been. "I can't tell you much."

"Because he's a SEAL and has an oath of secrecy. And he's sworn to keep silent even if his life is in danger and the people he cares about want to know if he's okay," Ruthie grumbled as she pushed through the men that'd crowded in around us.

"So…when did that happen?" Torren asked with a smile on his face.

I grinned. "Last night."

"Priorities, man. At least you've got them!" Torren winked.

I laughed.

It felt good to do that.

I hadn't been able to do it much this last month and a half.

In fact, it'd been quite solemn while we were there.

My team and I knew how bad it was.

Knew that we'd have to fight for our lives if we wanted to get out of there and ever return home again.

So yeah, smiling and laughing had been at a minimum.

Ruthie walked into the kitchen, and I watched her go, only realizing when I turned around that all eyes were on me.

"So…that's why you didn't stay last night," Silas said from behind me.

I turned slowly, seeing the man I looked up to beyond all others standing directly behind me with his arms crossed over his chest, and a very pissed off look in his eye.

Guess I didn't get past him like I'd originally thought.

That didn't surprise me, though.

Silas was a difficult man to read.

I still, to this day, had yet to figure out what he actually did.

I was aware that he owned quite a few businesses, and had his fingers in quite a few pies…but I knew he was more than that.

He had too many resources for him not to be…something.

I was betting he was CIA, but there was a bet going around that said he was a spy.

Whatever he was, I didn't really give a fuck…as long as he was at my back.

"I don't know what you're talking about," I hedged, mimicking his stance.

His eyes narrowed on me, then suddenly he took two giant steps forward and picked me up in a bear hug so tight that I could hardly breathe.

There were exactly four men in this world that could touch me like this.

That was Parker, Cormac, Garrison…and Silas.

And Silas had only done this to me twice.

The first time had been when I'd gotten initiated into the club and I finally received my patch.

The second was now.

And I took it as a sign…one that meant he'd missed me.

"I'm okay," I told him, slapping him on his back.

"I saw that for myself yesterday, and you look even better today. Which I'm guessing has something to do with that gray eyed, strawberry blonde who has a continuously bad attitude," Silas said. "And if you hurt her, you know I'll have to beat the shit out of you, right?"

I snorted.

Yet, I didn't doubt it whatsoever.

I knew for a fact that he'd be carrying out any and all punishments if I hurt his wife's best friend, and I respected him for it.

Ruthie needed someone like Silas on her side.

And I was glad she had it.

"I know," I nodded. "And you have my permission to if I do..."

He slapped his hand down a little harder than he needed to against my shoulder, and stepped back. "How about a round of shots as a celebration for making it home?"

I grinned.

"Sounds like a motherfuckin' plan."

Silas nodded, but gestured to a room at my back.

"We'll do it in church," he said. "I have some things I want you to know."

I narrowed my eyes at him.

What did he have to say that he wanted us to go to a place that was sacred to The Dixie Wardens?

Was something wrong?

Had something happened while I was away?

***

Ruthie

I poured ten more shots and placed them each on a simple black tray.

When I'd first started out at Halligans and Handcuffs, I'd been a complete novice when it came to drinks.

Now, long months later, I could practically recite each drink's alcohol content and exactly what it took to make it.

For instance, I knew that a 'Sex on The Beach' was made of one and a half ounces of vodka, half an ounce of peach Schnapps, two ounces of cranberry juice, and two ounces of orange juice.

If you'd ask me what ingredients had been in that when I'd started, I'd have blushed like a goddamned virgin, then stammered my way into ordering you a cocktail that I couldn't even say the name of to the bartender on duty.

Now, though, as the pretty brunette with pale blue eyes snottily said, "You do know what that is, don't you? Or have you never experienced something that amazing before?"

Then she'd proceeded to laugh in my face, and turn to hang all over the man that'd been in my bed only hours before, making me scream his name.

"Be nice, Naughty," Sterling reprimanded gently.

My eyes nearly crossed as I turned on my heels and ordered a 'Sex on the Beach' from Zander Cole, our hottie firefighter bartender for the night.

Zander was new, having joined the fire department straight out of college.

He looked like a wide-eyed flower child with his long blonde hair, blasé attitude, and smile that he gave damn near everyone.

Only it seemed to widen ever so slightly when I was near.

And when I ordered the drink, he blushed scarlet, but nonetheless made the drink for me.

I glanced up when I heard Sterling laugh.

I was so mad that I could spit nails.

He'd been my Sterling only hours before.

But when he'd gotten here, and his 'brothers', as he called them, surrounded him, he'd completely done a one eighty.

They'd disappeared for well over an hour, and the minute he got back, he started sucking back shots like they were water.

He was on his eighth (yes I'd counted) shot.

"Here you go," Zander said. "One Sex on the Beach."

Giving Zander a smile, I grabbed the stupid cocktail glass from the bar counter and started to walk in the direction of Sterling.

Audie, or 'Naughty' as Sterling had been calling her all night, took the drink I'd set down in front of her and took a long swallow, pulling the straw out with her teeth in an erotic gesture.

I wanted to claw her eyes out, but the worst thing was the way Sterling wasn't even acknowledging me.

And as I tried, yet again, to catch Sterling's eye, I realized that I wasn't going to.

Not tonight.

Sighing in frustration at Sterling and his ability to ignore everything about me, I finally decided that maybe it was a good time to go ahead and leave for the night.

My shift had ended over twenty minutes ago, but I'd stayed since the bar apparently wasn't closing at its usual time.

But the longer I stayed watching Audie drape herself over Sterling, and Sterling not push her away, I realized that just maybe I'd made a mistake.

Maybe I should leave after all.

Maybe this could be something we'd be able to talk about tomorrow.

I could only hope that Sterling was aware of the woman that was trying to do just about anything to get his attention.

And I also hoped that he was faithful.

Not that I'd asked him to be.

We hadn't done much talking when we were together this past night.

Yet, I'd thought a lot into it.

Maybe what was on his mind about us was something totally different than what I saw.

Walking back to the bar, I handed my tips and receipts to Silas who was standing at the end of the bar.

He had a bottle of Zigenbock in his hand, and he was staring out over his establishment with a sense of accomplishment and satisfaction covering his face.

"I'm cashing out," I told him.

He took my apron and nodded. "Mind if I get it back to you in the morning?"

I shook my head. "No, that's fine. I'll get it tomorrow after my shift at the gas station."

He nodded. "Going home?"

I nodded. "Yeah, I have to be up early tomorrow. I have a lunch date."

He smiled. "Sawyer told me you and Lily were having lunch"

I nodded. "Yeah, I seem to have created a monster friendship with the three of us."

He laughed. "Well, I appreciate you bringing her into the fold. Seeing her so happy makes me happy."

I grinned. "Later, gator."

"After a while, crocodile."

With that parting greeting, I headed out to my car, sighing heavily when I realized I didn't bring it.

Motherfucker.

***

I started walking home.

But ended up catching a ride with Mr. Adams, of all people.

Why he was out so early/late in the day I didn't know, but I was grateful.

"You shouldn't be walking home in the dark, girl," Mr. Adams said reproachfully.

I shrugged.

"Forgot my car today," I said.

"How do you 'forget your car?'" His old, grizzled voice asked with amusement.

I shrugged. "I don't want to talk about it, how about that?"

He nodded. "Fair enough, but next time, just say that instead of lying. Because it sounds like you're a shit liar, and there's no point in even trying to lie if you suck that bad."

"Yes, sir," I said. "Why are you out so late?"

"It's early, not late. And I'm going to my fishing hole," he answered.

I looked at the clock that now read three oh three A.M.

"This early?" I asked incredulously.

He nodded. "Gotta go sane for some bait fish, then I'm heading out on my boat to catch Big Blue."

"Who's Big Blue?" I asked. "And what's a 'sane?'"

He smiled at me.

"You 'sane' for batfish by using a huge throw net. As for 'blue's, they're catfish, darlin.' Ain't you ever heard of 'em called 'Blue's'?" he asked.

I shook my head. "I've never been fishing before. In fact, I've never even had the desire to fish."

He gave me a raised brow.

"Oh, really? Well it's said that you should give everything a try once. You never know if you'll like it," he said.

I shrugged. "I don't have anyone to go fishing with. I've spent my entire life inside. I wouldn't know the first thing about fishing."

"Ask that man of yours, I'm sure he knows how," Mr. Adams said.

Pain shot through my chest as I thought about 'that man' of mine.

"I'm mad at him. Let's not talk about him right now," I said, hoping to change the subject.

Mr. Adams laughed. "What'd he do?"

"Ignored me all night and kept letting a blonde bimbo touch him constantly," I muttered darkly.

Mr. Adams laughed. "You just said this morning that he was in the military. And it looked like he recently got home, too."

"How do you know he recently got home?" I asked suspiciously.

He looked at me with his old, knowing eyes.

"Clocked him the minute he got out of that storage room. His eyes were on everything all at once, and he held himself differently. Not to mention he categorized every single sound in the place," he answered. "When the ice machine kicked on in the back of the store, his eyes flashed there. Then you made a loud screeching sound as you drug the box of straws over the counter, causing him to flinch and look at you. His eyes kept bobbing back and forth to the door, to you, to me. Those actions only speak of a man that *had* to have those reactions to stay alive."

I shrugged. "And what's that got to do with anything I said?"

He gave me a droll look. "It may or may not have anything to do with 'it.' Whatever his problem may be. But you need to realize that things are going to be intensified. Reactions stronger, anger swifter, sorrow greater. Until he gets acclimated to being on US soil again, he's going to act a lot differently than he did before."

I thought about that for a long moment, and then decided that maybe he was right.

Whatever was said in the room beyond the bar tonight had affected him.

He'd been in a great mood earlier in the day.

Then all of a sudden he'd turned a one eighty, and hadn't even looked at me all night except for covert glances when he thought I wasn't looking.

But not once had he said a word to me after he stepped foot out of that room.

"Whatever," I finally said.

I didn't really want to talk about this.

Being rational about it wasn't helping.

I wasn't a 'rational' thinking kind of person.

I'd always thought with my heart.

Which equaled more 'seat of my pants' kind of reactions.

"Come with me tonight. I'll take you to my pond," he said suddenly.

I blinked, turning to him to study his face.

The green light from his dash lit up his paper-thin skin, and outlined the wrinkles, causing dark shadows to appear.

"I can't," I said reluctantly. "Can I come sometime soon, though? I think I'd like to learn how."

He nodded. "You know where I live."

I nodded again, and turned as the truck came to a bouncing stop in front of my house.

I didn't bother to ask him how he knew where I lived.

Everyone knew where I lived.

It was the talk of the town about the convict living in the nice 'burb of Benton.

"Okay, Mr. Adams. Thank you for the ride," I said, opening my door.

However, when my feet both met the pavement outside my home, Mr. Adams stopped me.

"You know," he said. "There was this one time with my Annie that I was really upset. I'd had a really bad day at work, and I wanted to talk to her. However, she was too busy doing something else, and a neighbor woman came over to offer my Annie a pie. Well, the neighbor lady and I got to talking, and my Annie came out spitting mad because I was talking to another woman that wasn't her. You wanna know why I did it?"

I shook my head.

But my answer was the opposite of what I was feeling.

"Why did you do it?" I asked softly.

He smiled, looking far away into a memory that I couldn't see.

"Because I knew she'd fight for me. She may have been busy, but I knew all I had to do was talk to that woman, and she'd get un-busy. Because that's my Annie. She was possessive and I liked her that way. Which begs to question…why didn't you do something?"

I looked at him for a long time, wondering the same thing.

Why hadn't I done something?

Why hadn't I forced the issue?

And as I fell asleep that night, upset now at myself and not him, I realized two things.

One, I was in love with Sterling.

And two, I needed to fight for him if he was what I wanted.

Because he deserved to be fought for.

CHAPTER 8

Be patriotic. Show your boobies to a veteran.
-T-shirt

Ruthie

I walked out on my front porch the next morning, hoping beyond hope that my newspaper was there, and was startled to see a man on my porch reading it.

"Thanks for getting it," I said, yanking the offending paper out of his hand and going back inside.

My paper was stolen from my front lawn four out of seven days a week, and I was just happy that it was there.

What I wasn't happy with was Sterling being on my front porch.

I'd had time to reconnect with my anger after I'd called him three times this morning.

I would've slammed the door, but Sterling's body was just suddenly *there*.

"Get out," I said as I continued walking, smoothing the paper back in its original folded position before laying it on the kitchen table next to my coffee.

I sat down and arranged myself, picking up my Pop-Tart and taking a bite as I started to scan the first page.

I loved reading the paper.

It was so nice to know what was going on around me.

Something I'd become used to in the days since I'd been released from prison.

"I forgot my phone at home, and you weren't answering your door. Where were you?" He asked me.

I looked up from my paper with half my Pop-Tart remaining.

"I was out in the backyard tending my garden," I informed him.

He nodded. "I've been sitting on the porch for two hours now. Wish I would've known you were out back the whole time."

I sighed.

"I was trying to be mad at you," I told him.

His brows rose.

"Why?" He asked, genuinely confused.

"Because of that girl, Audie, hanging over you all night last night," I said.

His head tilted sideways.

"I don't remember anybody named Audie," he finally answered.

I raised a brow. "Yeah, that makes sense. You were drunk off your ass, though."

He shrugged.

"You're not even going to tell me what had you so upset last night?" I continued.

He tilted his head, first one way and then the other, cracking it loudly before starting on his fingers.

The movement made the muscles in his forearm jump and release, drawing my attention to the way his shirt fit him.

There was no gap whatsoever in the entire t-shirt.

His jeans fit him well, too.

Too well.

Because then I started thinking about the things I wanted to do to him instead of the things he'd done yesterday to upset me.

He began, going straight to the problem at hand.

"A couple of years ago, when I first got into The Dixie Wardens," Sterling said, sucking back half a glass of water before he turned to me, pinning me to the spot. "I asked Silas to look for someone."

I nodded. "Yeah, that's what I got from what I overheard."

He didn't look surprised that I knew something about what he was trying to tell me, only resigned.

"I stopped looking for her when I realized that she was under someone's protection, and that someone's protection was good. Good enough that I couldn't crack it without being put on radar, and having her put on radar as well," he informed me. "Silas was the one doing the looking, and he'd told me what he'd found out within a week of me asking it of him. But not wanting to disturb it any more than I'd already done, I told him to back off. Except he's been keeping tabs on my mom all these years."

"Okay," I said. "So what did Silas have to say that upset you so much?"

"Told me that she got here in Louisiana a little over a day ago, and that her new husband was with her," he rumbled, staring down at his toes.

Or his cock.

I really couldn't tell which.

They were both in the same direction he was looking.

"So what's the big deal with that?" I asked.

He sighed.

"Not a 'big deal' per se, but more of an inconvenience," he admitted, pulling his hands up until they rested on top of his head, fingers interlaced on top.

"I'm not seeing the problem," I finally said.

He sighed.

And I was really confused.

What was the big deal with his mom being here? Hell, I could see why it'd be a big deal why my mom was here, but hadn't he grown up with his?

"My mom gave me up when I was a kid," he said finally.

My mouth about hit the floor.

"You're fucking *kidding* me," I said.

He shook his head. "No."

"You're telling me that we have foster care in common and you never said a word?" I practically yelled.

He shrugged, and suddenly I was extremely pissed off.

I'd told him multiple times about how I'd been given up when I was a young girl. How hard it'd been, and how I wouldn't wish it upon anyone. Knowing that you once belonged to someone, then having them decide that they no longer wanted you, was a killer on a person's heart.

I always felt so alienated about it.

Yet, low and behold, the same fucking thing had happened to him!

Wouldn't that be something you'd share?

I mean, where was the fucking camaraderie?

Weren't fucked up kids supposed to commiserate with other fucked up kids just like them?

And didn't the same go for adults?

Apparently, it didn't work like that for Sterling.

And I found myself mostly disappointed.

I always felt so alone.

It was a terrible thing to have your mother tell you when you were ten years old that 'you're not worth the trouble.'

I never knew my dad well.

And from what I'd been able to gather when I was younger, my father never even knew I was his kid.

My mom had hid it from him.

Why, I couldn't tell you.

My dad had been rather wealthy from what I understood, and my mom hadn't been.

Personally, I would've put my own happiness aside and made sure that my child had a chance to know his or her father.

Hell, I did do that very thing.

"I don't like talking about it," he finally said, jarring me out of my own personal hell.

That road never led to the correct path.

It always led to despair and sorrow.

And I was tired of being on that road.

"You're either going to have to stop acting like it's a big deal, or talk to me. Because all you're doing right now with the bad attitude is pissing me off and making me even more curious," I told him.

I could hear his teeth grind, then he growled in frustration.

"I'm still pissed off about it, alright? It pisses me off that she's fucking happy, while I've spent nearly my entire life fucked over. Shouldn't she be fucking miserable because I had to be?" He all but yelled.

I blinked.

"No. She is your mother. Everyone deserves to be happy. Does that make our anger rational, though? Hell no. It doesn't. That's what a human being does. Our emotions control us. Which was why I killed my husband for killing my daughter, then had to spend nearly nine years in prison," I told him.

He didn't laugh like I'd intended.

"You're husband deserved to die," he informed me. "I still can't believe you had to serve any time at all."

I shrugged. "It was worth it."

Did that make me a bad person, wanting my husband dead for what he did to me? To our unborn baby?

Because if it did, I didn't really care.

I could still feel a hole in my heart.

Still feel how much it hurt to see other people having babies left and right.

"I've been looking for my father for a long time myself, but I don't have resources like you do," I told him.

He blinked. "Why are you looking for your father?"

I fiddled with the crust of my Pop-Tart, breaking it off as I said, "I don't think my father knew who I was. He was always so nice to me when he saw my mom, but he never knew who I was to him. I don't know if he'd even care to know me now…after what I did. Which is why I haven't gone further than just doing my own searches on the internet."

"I don't know why you think you did something wrong. Do you know how many times I thought about killing the people who beat on my mom? Or even my foster parents? It was the worst existence anybody could think of for a kid. I daydreamed about ways to kill them and make it look like an accident," he told me, crossing his arms over his chest.

"You were a kid," I told him.

He shrugged. "So fucking what? I was eighteen when I left that place, and I still wished they'd be hit by a car and killed on their way home to drop me off at the airport."

I smothered a laugh.

"One day you'll have to give me more information on what they did to you. But right now we need to discuss what the big deal about your mom being in the same city as you," I told him. "What's it matter if she does know? Don't you think she'll want to see you?"

He said something so softly, that I had to move closer and ask him to repeat himself.

"I said I don't want her to be disappointed in me. How I've lived my life," he answered roughly.

I glanced at the ceiling to make sure the roof wasn't caving in. *Had I hear him right?*

"Sterling…" I started. "You're in the Navy. You're a freakin' SEAL. You're a mother lovin' hero. Why wouldn't she be proud of you?"

He shrugged, and I finally saw the vulnerability in his actions.

His words.

"Honey, she'll love you," I told him.

And if she didn't, I'd kill her.

What was another ten years?

Okay, maybe it wouldn't be just ten years this time. Second offenses usually weren't looked upon too openly.

Maybe I'd just beat her up.

Kick her ass some, and let her know what she'd lost by acting like an ass and not loving her son like he deserved.

Then again, I kind of felt that way about her already.

I would've gone through hell to keep my child.

Which, in essence, might have been what she'd done to keep him safe.

Shit, now I couldn't be mad at her.

"What's that look on your face for?" Sterling asked suspiciously.

I shrugged, moving from my seat and walking to him.

He opened his arms, and I face planted into his muscular chest, rubbing my face between his pectorals.

"That's kind of like motorboating…" he observed.

I laughed and lifted my hands to place both of my hands on his pecs.

They were so well defined that I could practically bounce a quarter off them.

And don't even get me started on his freakin' abs.

Those were just ungodly perfect.

"What are you thinking about?" Sterling asked, his hand moving up until it wrapped around my throat.

His fingers came to a stop at the frantic pounding of my pulse at the base of my jaw, and I closed my eyes as Sterling realized what he was doing to me.

"You have a way that really calls to every primal level of me," he said, backing me up until my ass met the kitchen table.

I could do nothing but lay back on it as he continued to push me forward until my back bowed over the table.

His hand was still at my neck, and my eyes fluttered closed as I felt the raw power of everything that was Sterling.

His hand tightened slightly as his fingers started to trail along the hem of my tiny shorts that I'd thrown on this morning.

His fingers dipped underneath them, and he realized rather quickly that I wasn't wearing anything underneath since he met skin and slickness.

I shaved everything that I could from my shoulders down.

It sucked major ass not to shave whenever I wanted to, and the moment I was able to, I shaved absolutely everything, and kept it cleaned so I didn't have a single prickly spot on my body.

It's pure torture to be dictated on what you can and can't do grooming wise.

But what was more torturous was the way Sterling's tongue licked along the seam of my lips, making them part to his tongue like the wanton slut I was.

Our hands became tangled as we started to remove the other's clothes.

He started with my shirt, pleasantly surprised to see my breasts exposed the moment my shirt was free of my shoulders.

The next thing to go was Sterling's belt.

His gun that was at the small of his back was placed on the table, caught before it could tumble to the floor in my exuberance.

The next thing to go was his skintight black t-shirt, followed shortly by my shorts.

I hissed when my overheated pussy met the cool laminate of my breakfast table, and I made a mental note to get some bleach spray and wipe it down later.

But that thought got lost in the bombard of pure perfection when Sterling leaned forward and pulled my nipple into his hungry mouth.

He sucked hard, pulling so ravenously at my nipple that I cried out in a little bit of pain and a lot of excitement.

Pleasure started to rocket through my system as I shook with each hard pull of his mouth.

My hands found his hair as I fell backwards, and he came with me, staying connected with me all the way down.

Once my back hit the cool table, he let go of my nipple with a pop, and placed small, wet kisses all the way down to my eager pussy.

Once he reached the top of my slit, he turned his eyes up to me, placed both hands firmly on my hips, and slowly started to lap at my clit.

My eyes rolled back in my head as his talented tongue showed me everything he could do.

My knees came up on their own volition, coming to a rest on the very edge of the table as my hands went back down to his hair, holding on for dear life.

Each lash of his tongue had my hips jolting upwards, but Sterling's strong grip on my hips had me holding steady even when I didn't want to.

"Fuck," I said, somewhat breathily.

Okay, a whole lot breathily.

I sounded like a fucking freight train billowing steam as my orgasm started to rush at me like a freakin' wrecking ball bursting through a flimsy falling down building.

And the moment he thrust two strong, thick fingers into my wet heat, I detonated, exploding into a million tiny pieces and screaming his name at the top of my lungs.

"Sterling!" I shrieked.

He chuckled darkly against the lips of my sex, and before I could even blink, he was there.

Pulling his shorts down in jerky yanks, shoving his underwear down far enough that his cock and balls fell free, and lined himself up with my entrance.

I pulled my knees back, giving him an unhindered view of what he was about to have, and he growled. An evil smirk tilted up the corner of his mouth just before he slammed inside of me.

My eyes fell shut and I lost the grip on my thighs as my hands came down to the lip of the table while I held on for dear life.

I'd realized in the time that Sterling had spent with me in this capacity that he was not a 'gentle' kind of man.

He was a *fuck hard* kind of man.

And I liked it.

I liked how he held nothing back and gave me everything he had.

It was freeing to know he trusted me that much to give me his all.

And give me all he did, and then some.

"I like how your breasts jump each time I shove my cock into you," he groaned, eyes dancing from my breasts to where we were connected.

The roughness of his thrusts had my kitchen table moving, and before long we'd moved it from where it'd been, in the middle of the floor, until it was butted up against the counter.

I would've laughed had I not been too busy trying to catch my breath.

But then he suddenly just stopped, pulling out and smacking the outside of my thigh.

"Turn over, feet on the floor and hips against the edge of the table," he ordered roughly.

I did as he asked, prying my fingers loose from the table edge and rolling, knocking off my nearly empty glass of milk in the process.

I barely even noticed the spill, seeing as Sterling wasted no time filling me back up.

I groaned and pressed my forehead against the table, hands going up to press against the sides of the counter trying to counteract his hard thrusts.

My hips felt slightly uncomfortable, but the pleasure starting to bloom deep in my belly counteracted any and all pain until everything I felt was nothing but ecstasy.

Stroke after stroke of his cock plowing into me, the *smack-smack* of his hips hitting my ass, as well as the wet sound of our joining as his cock slid in and out of my needy hole had my orgasm all of a sudden *there*.

Not to mention his balls kept swinging to hit my clit just perfectly.

"Oh, fuck," I breathed into the tabletop.

His dark, amused chuckle had me seeing stars when he changed the angle of his strokes, making my previously amazing orgasm vault out of orbit into the extremes that I'd never felt before.

The breath left my lungs in a choked gasp, and his hand came up to hold onto the top of my shoulder, squeezing tightly, as his orgasm overtook him.

I could feel the hot pulses of his come pouring into me, splashing against the back of my womb, and I screamed.

It was muffled by the tabletop, but I couldn't find it in myself to care whether I disturbed the neighbors or not.

I couldn't even remember my own name by that point.

"Goddamn," Sterling said as he collapsed against my back.

What little breath I'd been able to catch left my lungs in a whoosh when his body met mine, and he laughed at the small squeak that came out of me in the process.

"Sorry," he said, lifting until his elbows held him up.

I grunted in answer, turning my head to the side and allowing my body to catch the breath it needed after that spectacular show.

"Your cock is welcome in me anytime," I told him jokingly.

The cock in question jerked at my announcement, and he pressed his bushy beard against my neck as he ran his lips along my shoulder blades.

"Good to know," he said, reaching forward and grabbing something off the counter in front of me.

My eyes followed the movement as he unceremoniously shoved the towel underneath my pubic bone where it rested on the table.

Then he pulled out, and a rush of his release started to instantly flow out.

"Convenient that you fucked me over here," I said, placing the dishtowel to my opening and catching what I could before it ended up all over the floor and my thighs.

"I'm a multitasker," he said, a grin playing along his lips. "What are you doing today?"

I tried not to be embarrassed by the fact that I was completely naked on my kitchen table and he was acting like I wasn't.

"I have to go to lunch with Sawyer today," I answered. "And tonight I have to start getting ready…"

My next comment was interrupted by a no-nonsense knock at the door, and I knew exactly who was out there.

I'd been getting visits from the police nearly every three days since Sterling had left.

And that sounded like Officer Ryan's knock.

He wasn't the nicest cop, but he also wasn't harsh like some of them could be.

He was honest, which sadly equaled into me getting a ticket if I'd done something he deemed as wrong.

"Shit," I said, hopping down and waddling to the door. "Can you get that? Might want to do your pants up first, though. Tell him I'll be out in a minute."

His eyes narrowed, but he pulled up his jeans, fixed his belt and holster, and walked to the front door shirtless just as I closed the door behind me.

CHAPTER 9

A giant cup of shut the fuck up.
-Coffee cup

Sterling

I opened the door, surprised to see a cop on the other side of it.

"Can I help you?" I asked, scratching my beard.

The cop looked me up and down, cataloged my tattoos. The gun that I'd tucked inside its holster at the small of my back just as I'd opened the door. The scowl on my face.

Then instantly took a step back.

One predator knew another when they saw each other.

"Is Ms. Comalsky home?" He asked briskly.

I raised a brow at him.

"She's getting dressed," I told him, crossing my arms over my chest.

His eyes flicked behind me, looking for her, before he turned back to me.

"What's your name," he demanded.

Not a question, very much a demand.

But I knew my rights, and I didn't have to tell him a damn thing. And I wasn't liking the way he was being so rude, and challenging me in my woman's house.

"My name's none of your business," I said just as Ruthie came up behind

127

me.

"Officer Ryan," she said the moment she came up behind me.

She pressed her face against my bare arm, wrapping both hands around my arm.

I wasn't sure whether she was doing it because she could tell I was pissed, or because she wanted to just hold my hand.

Whatever the reason, I was happy for it.

I liked the possessive action coming from her.

Any other woman and it would've pissed me off, but Ruthie was mine. And she could have me. Touch me. Do anything she fucking wanted to me and I'd allow it.

Officer Ryan's eyes narrowed, and it was then I saw that he was attracted to Ruthie.

His eyes had dilated the moment she'd come into the room, and then darkened when he saw how she was holding on to me.

And I knew the second he decided he was going to be a dick.

He pulled out a piece of paper from his pocket and handed it to her. "Didn't want it to get wet this time."

Ruthie took it from his outstretched hand and crumbled it in her hands.

"Thanks," she said through gritted teeth.

I took the crumpled piece of paper from her hand and scanned it quickly while Officer Ryan turned his back to us and started down the walk in the rain.

I followed him out the moment I realized she was getting a ticket.

The water hit my chest and started to slide down my skin in cool rivulets, but I couldn't even contemplate that right then because I was so goddamned pissed.

It was likely steam was pouring off my skin with how mad I was.

I looked first left down the street, then right.

In those two glances, I saw eight cars, three on the left, and five on the right.

"Did you give them tickets, too?" I asked.

He didn't say anything, only started towards his car.

Rage boiling in my gut, I pulled out my phone and hit Loki's face on the screen.

"Yeah?" Loki asked roughly.

He sounded like he'd been sleeping.

But I didn't care right then.

"I'm about to fight a cop…" I said, making the cop walking away from me freeze. "How many years in prison is it if I hurt him?"

"Threatening one'll get you prison time, too. Where are you?" He asked, sounding more alert now.

"I'm at Ruthie's. And this isn't a fuckin' threat. This is real life, *I'm going to bust his face in*, seriousness," I spat.

"I'll be there in ten."

I bet it was more like five, but I didn't contradict him.

I also knew he'd be calling in backup.

The rain started to pour down harder, and my pants really started to get soaked.

My phone would probably be fried shortly, too.

Yet that didn't bother me.

I was so fucking tired of Ruthie being treated like shit.

Beyond tired of it.

I was tired of it three months ago, and it split me in two to know she'd been dealing with this while I was gone.

"So tell me," I snarled. "Did you give all of them tickets, too?"

The officer looked wary.

His hand was hovering close to his gun as if he was ready to go for it at any second.

And his eyes were watching me like I was a poisonous snake ready to strike.

"I can't divulge that information," he answered smoothly.

I smiled. "You can't, can you?"

My eyes perked when I heard motorcycles heading towards us, and I smiled.

Which made the jerkoff in front of me step back.

This time he rested the palm of his hand on the butt of his gun.

"You gonna go for that without reason?"

"All I have to do is fear for my life, and there's my reason," he answered.

"Do you fear for your life?" I asked him.

He didn't answer.

The motorcycles that'd been coming towards us finally stopped, but I didn't look at them.

You didn't take your eyes off a target that was ready to shoot.

"What's going on here?"

Loki.

"Officer?"

Silas.

"Sterling, what the fuck is going on?"

Cleo.

I smiled darkly at the officer, and his eyes narrowed.

"Y'all need to back up and step back to your bikes. There's no reason you need to be here," Officer Dickhead said.

"Actually, these are my brothers," I said. "And they have every right to be here."

"Not right now they don't. I'll call in back up if you don't get on your motorcycles right now and leave," he growled.

I was completely soaked to the bone when I heard the first siren.

And it was obvious the second Officer Ryan heard the first siren, that he was relieved to be having backup.

I had a feeling he didn't know what kind of connection that I had, nor who and what I was.

Because if he had, he would've known that it was futile to try anything with me.

The Dixie Wardens owned this town.

Something he found out when Trance finally showed.

Loki caught his eye and gestured forward.

When they both got to my side, they turned to stare at Officer Ryan like he wasn't playing on their team.

"Officer," Loki said. "What's going on?"

Officer Ryan looked from me, to Loki, to Trance, then back to Loki before saying, "Gave the woman a ticket for parking overnight. He wouldn't let it go."

He pointed me out like I was a schoolyard bully, and it made me want to laugh my ass off.

I managed to suppress it, though.

Instead I crossed my arms over my slippery chest and waited.

And it didn't take long.

"What do you mean you gave her a ticket for overnight parking?" Loki asked.

Officer Ryan sneered at Loki.

"She was illegally parked," he defended.

Loki looked up and down the street and pointed at several different cars.

"Did they get tickets?" He asked.

"No."

"Why not?" Trance asked.

Officer Ryan sneered. "Because they weren't there all night."

"How do you know she was there all night?" Trance countered.

"Because I came at the beginning and end of my shift," he said. "She was there both times."

"But you don't know that she was there all night. It could be that she was there when you came, left in between, and came and parked once again," Trance said.

"In the exact same spot?" Officer Ryan countered.

"Well, you can't prove that she didn't move, unless you have video surveillance of it. Not to mention you started shift at ten at night, and it's only just now sun up," Loki said. "And if you didn't give these people over here tickets," he indicated the cars with a pointed finger. "Then that's not fair and equal treatment."

Let's just say, it only digressed from there.

Thirty minutes later, the entire city block was the proud new owner of a parking ticket, and the neighborhood drivers who were unlucky enough to park in the road were not happy campers.

Especially the ones I assumed called in the first place.

There were a trio of women staring at us from the front porch, two houses down, and I could tell from the way they were pointing and sneering that they thought this was a joke.

But Silas and Loki hadn't been joking.

And the chief wasn't joking.

Since Ryan refused to take back the ticket, he was forced to give one to everyone he saw parked overnight, and that was something easily resolved by pulling his dashboard cam.

"You shouldn't have done that," Ruthie said quietly at my side.

I wrapped my arm around her shoulder and pulled her into my side.

"I know," I said.

And I did.

It would only make the entire situation worse.

Way worse.

"I have to go to lunch," she whispered. "Do I go pay the ticket on the way home?"

"I wouldn't," I said. "The officer has to send his paperwork in, and my guess would be he won't turn any of this paperwork in at all. It would be too much work for him to. And I bet every one of you protest the ticket. The law is stupid and shouldn't have been made into one in the first place. It's too hard to enforce it."

She nodded at my side.

"So I just wait for the information in the mail to see if they process it?" She asked.

I nodded. "That's what I would do."

"Okay," she said. "Can I get out of here without hitting anybody?"

"I'll pull it out for you," I said.

She was boxed in on three sides. The back side with bikes, the front side with a cruiser, the left side by the curb, and the right side by Trance's K-9 unit.

She handed me the keys to her car, and I had to laugh at the sheer amount of key chains she had on it.

"You know," I said. "This isn't good for your ignition to have a key chain this heavy hanging from it."

She glared at me.

"I don't remember asking your opinion on the state of my steering column," she griped, turning on her heel and walking back into her house.

"Testy," Loki said.

I nodded. "She's upset that I butted my 'fat head' into the problem and made it 'ten times fucking worse.'"

I used air quotes as I repeated what she'd said to me, causing him to laugh.

"Sounds like a good woman you have there. Better hold onto her," Loki said.

I winked at him.

"Plan to."

"Come down to the station and let the chief know what happened for me. He wants to keep on top of it. Says we may need to call the PAR officer out here," Loki said, looking up at the rain.

We were standing under the awning of Ruthie's front porch now that it was raining harder than it had been, waiting for the rest of the officers that'd been called in as backup by the neighbors to disperse.

Not to mention riding a motorcycle in the rain wasn't something that we did if we didn't have to.

And apparently they were all off today.

"Okay," I said.

I didn't like the PAR officer for this area; she was rude and treated everyone like they were beneath her.

She also hated me because we'd been in the same foster home. For a year, at least.

If she'd only known how bad Garrison, Cormac, and I had had it, she wouldn't hate me.

Except she didn't know.

She was blissfully unaware because she was the chosen foster child.

The one kid that never got beaten.

That never had to do chores.

She thought we were always getting to go out with our 'foster dad.'

What she didn't know was that when she thought we were 'going out,' we were actually getting the shit beaten out of us one at a time.

When she thought we used to go get drunk, we were actually so beaten to shit and back that we couldn't walk straight.

"I'm not calling that bitch. She can go fuck herself. I'll move Ruthie out of here before she gets involved," I growled.

"She's already involved," an amused woman's voice said from in front of us.

I wanted to throw Ruthie's five pounds of key chains at her.

Instead, I closed my eyes and counted to ten.

When that didn't work, I counted to twenty.

Then I walked inside and slammed the door.

Ruthie was standing there, eyes wide.

She looked to be close to coming out of the house, almost as if her fingers had been on the door handle, and she'd jumped back when I'd thrown it open.

"What's going on?" She asked.

"The devil's on your front porch and I don't want to talk to her," I answered, leaning my back against the door.

Ruthie's eyes roamed down my chest, stopping at the bulge in my pants that seemed to come alive anytime she was near.

"I thought the devil was a man," she said lazily, moving closer to me.

I shook my head. "All devils are women."

"How do you know?" She teased, leaning into me.

Her soft breasts pressed into my diaphragm, and I inhaled swiftly, drinking her scent in.

"Because women are the torturers. Men can torture, but women know how to do it *wayyy* better than men," I answered her, snaking my arm around her back and pulling her into me roughly.

"And what's this devil ever done to you?" She asked.

"The devil, her name is Thomasina Daniels, and she made the last year of my life a living hell on an island of viperous snakes, with a constant firestorm devouring it. I'd describe it as worse than hell," I informed her.

Her lips moved forward until they hovered over mine.

"And what are we going to do about her being out there?" She asked. "What'll make her go away?"

"Nothing," I answered honestly.

It was honest, too.

Brutally honest.

I avoided the bitch because she never left me the fuck alone when she saw me.

And I knew it'd take a miracle to get her to leave.

She took pride in fucking with me.

The bad thing was that I didn't really even know why.

"She won't go away at all?" She asked.

I shook my head. "No. She'll stay there until I get out, unless the boys convince her to go...and I don't think they're capable of convincing her of that."

"Well," she said, pulling out her phone and texting someone.

Her fingers moved expertly over the keyboard of her phone before she shoved it back in her purse and dropped her purse to the floor.

"What was that?" I asked worriedly.

"I texted the girls," she answered.

"Why?"

"Because I'm going to be late..." she said.

Then her mouth was on mine, and I forgot how to breathe.

"We can't..." I tried.

There were about ten people on the front porch only separated from us by a shitty front door.

They'd hear.

I knew they would.

Ruthie was too loud, and I was too rough to keep her from being loud.

"Sure we can," she said, her hands going to the buckle of my pants.

That was the easy part.

The rest was hard because my pants were still wet, sticking stiffly to my thighs and nearly impossible to remove since they were quite tight.

But she tried, and got my pants down to just about mid-thigh before she gave up.

"That's enough," she said. "I got what I want out."

I would've been more amused had she not taken that moment to drop to her knees and suck my entire cock into her mouth.

She swallowed the motherfucker, and I was completely hard.

I felt the back of her throat, and threw my head back in ecstasy.

"Holy fuck!" I exclaimed as the back of my head hit the door with a solid thud.

Ruthie laughed, and I felt that laugh in my feet.

"Fuck," I said again.

I was being really articulate, I knew.

But I could do nothing less.

The woman had the power to scramble my brains with just her mouth alone.

"Fuck, fuck, fuck," I continued as she started to bob her head.

And when she swallowed, making her throat muscles work on my cock head, I pulled her up by her armpits and spun around so her back hit the door with a solid *thwack*.

"Take me," she ordered as I ripped her shorts and panties down her legs.

I went down to my knees, bending as best I could with my wet jeans around the bend of my hips.

Although awkward, I managed to throw one of her legs over my shoulders, opening up her pussy to my starving mouth.

I didn't waste time fucking around, I went straight for the good stuff and latched on to her throbbing clit.

Her flavor burst onto my tongue, spreading through my system so fast that I could've come.

She wouldn't have liked that, though, and I would've been embarrassed.

So I dropped one hand to my throbbing cock and squeezed the head tightly as I started to suck on her clit.

When she yanked on my hair to force me lower, I took the hint and thrust my tongue inside of her pussy.

She was so wet that I slid straight inside, and my eyes rolled back at the honeyed taste of her.

I fucked her with my tongue, and she urged me on by using her hands in my hair.

And just when I felt her orgasm start to take over, I shot up, dropping her leg as I went.

She gasped in surprise, or annoyance at me for having stopped, but I didn't make her wait long before I fed my cock deep inside her pussy.

I didn't stop until I bottomed out inside of her.

Our hips met, and I lifted first one leg, then the other, until both circled around my back.

Then with little preamble, I started to fuck her.

Long, deep strokes.

I was taking her so hard that she bounced against the door.

However, my mind wasn't on the people on the other side of the door.

It was all on the woman that was staring into my eyes, looking at me like I was her world.

The only thing that mattered in hers was whether I was with her in it.

And that was something I'd never had from anybody else.

Sure, I had great friends, but the human mind has a certain protectiveness about it.

It always looks out for itself first, then others that you love.

Well, that wasn't what was in Ruthie's eyes right then.

It was all her love.

For me.

She wanted me to be happy.

And I wanted her to be happy over my own happiness.

Which was, I guessed, what made a real relationship, one that was true and pure, work.

"You stopped," she whispered, her hands framing my face.

I turned my head and kissed the palm of her hand.

"I have to tell you something…after we're done. Don't let me forget," I told her.

Her eyes widened. "Are you going to say you're breaking up with me and just getting this done before you do?"

My mouth dropped open.

"That was *not* what I was going to say…not even close!" I snapped.

She looked wary and I sighed, pressing into her even deeper, letting my cock and the weight of my body hold her up so I could raise my hands up to her face.

"I wanted to tell you I love you, but I thought it was a little cliché to do it while we were fucking," I snapped.

Her eyes narrowed.

"Well, you could call it something other than 'fucking.' That sounds tacky when in the same breath you told me you loved me," she snapped back.

I blinked.

"Well…?" I asked, waiting patiently.

"Well what?" She asked nonchalantly.

I dropped my hands from her face and grinned.

Well if that's the way she wanted to play it, I could deal with that.

Holding onto her ass, I withdrew my cock from her tight heat all the way before I slammed back inside.

It was a furious movement, in and out; so fast that I barely had time to realize I was out before I was back inside her.

She screamed.

Loudly.

Then she was coming.

Coming so hard that her pretty pussy clamped down on my cock, and I saw the heavens.

"Sweet, merciful mother of God…" I gasped.

She was so fucking tight.

"God, Sterling. Yes!" Ruthie cried. *"Yes!"*

I couldn't even function.

I was coming too, and I hadn't even been aware I was close.

Come shot out of my cock in long spurts, bathing her insides in my essence as she continued to call my name.

"Sterling," she gasped.

I growled as I started to work the last few dregs of come out of me, coming down from my orgasm gradually.

"You're like a freakin' drug," she whispered.

I buried my face in her neck before there was a loud pound on the door nearly on top of my face.

"I'm not going away, even after hearing how slutty you and your woman sound."

I stiffened and started to pull away when Ruthie's arms tightened around my neck.

"Go out the back," she whispered.

I pulled out of her wetly, smiling when my come started to leak out of her, falling to her thighs like an erotic picture.

She looked down, following my gaze, and laughed.

"You would find this sexy," she shook her head.

But when she would've walked to the bathroom, I stopped her with a hand in her hair.

"You forgot to say something," I whispered darkly.

She snorted.

"I didn't forget a damn thing," she answered, walking forward until I either let her hair go or hurt her.

I let her go.

But then she turned to look at me over her shoulder, dressed only in a shirt with her hair a messy mass around her face and over her shoulders.

"Sterling?" She asked.

I rose one brow at her. "Yeah?"

"You're gonna laugh," she admitted.

"Laugh at what?" I wondered aloud.

"I don't want to say I love you…because love screwed me over once and I don't know if I can ever say it again. Because those words lost meaning to me. But I…*ich liebe dich,*" she said before hurrying to the bathroom.

I followed her, stripping my wet pants off and kicking them against the far wall of her bedroom.

"What language is that?" I asked her softly, taking a seat on the bed so I could see her as she wet a washcloth in the sink.

Her head hung.

"It's something I remember my…dad…saying to someone on the phone. I looked it up one day. It means I love you in German," she whispered.

Almost so softly that I couldn't even hear her.

But it was enough.

For now, it was enough.

CHAPTER 10

It's a bend me over the bed and make me like it kind of day.
-Coffee Cup

Sterling

"Where's Ruthie?" Cormac asked me four hours later as we walked into the gas station.

I grimaced.

"She's having lunch with Sawyer," I told him. "You realize we're going to get covered in mud, don't you?"

Cormac shrugged. "Been done before, boy."

Garrison grabbed three Gatorades from the cooler and walked up to the checkout to pay.

"What's his problem?" I asked Cormac,

Cormac's eyes went to Garrison, then back to mine.

"He's still upset with you."

I froze and turned to survey Cormac's face. "What do you mean he's upset with me? Why? I haven't even been here to offend him."

He didn't say anything, only raised his brows at me for so long that I started to think over what I'd just said.

Then it hit me.

Literally.

"Here," Garrison said as he tossed a Gatorade at my chest.

It hit me with a thump and fell to the floor at my feet.

I looked up at Garrison to see his back retreating out the door, and I knew what I had to do.

I ran at him from behind, tackling him in the grass about thirty yards from the entrance.

He went down hard with me on his back, and I got him in a chokehold that he wouldn't be getting out of anytime soon.

"Get off me, ass fucker," Garrison growled, struggling uselessly to get me to off him.

I only held on, putting my face close enough to his that my beard was in his eye.

"I love you, fucker. And what's wrong with ass fucking?" I asked.

"Nothing's wrong with ass fucking, I just don't want it from you. Now get off me," he said, rolling onto his back.

I let go of him and Garrison was instantly on his feet.

"You look like shit," I said, studying him.

Garrison sighed.

"It's school. There's a new football coach that's riding my ass constantly. Not to mention that you've been missing for nearly ten weeks, and all of a sudden you show up, demanding we play ball with you like nothing even happened!" Garrison yelled, waving his hands in the air.

Garrison had always been a hand talker.

He acted out everything as he spoke, embellishing where shit needed embellished.

He was always overly animated, too.

Everything with Garrison got blown out of proportion.

But I didn't mind.

I loved Garrison like a brother, despite his annoying faults.

"Yeah, it was fun to drive two and a half hours thinking that something was really wrong," Cormac said, finally catching up to us.

He had all three Gatorades in his hands, as well as all three gloves.

The moment he got close enough, he started to divvy out our things, stopping only when he held his glove and Gatorade.

"So let's go do this. I have to be back by seven for a game," Cormac said.

I raised a brow at him, but nonetheless started to walk.

We usually played at the park right down the street from us, stopping in at the gas station for a drink along our way.

It was about twenty minutes from my place, and served as a central meeting point for the three of us.

"So what's up with the football coach? Is he being a dick on purpose?" I asked.

Garrison shook his head. "No. Yes. I don't fuckin' know. I think he's threatened by me. But I've never done a damn thing to him. I'm not even involved in the football team."

Garrison was the baseball coach at Shreveport High, and the lead science teacher.

He was a smart motherfucker, and maybe the guy was just threatened by him on a general level.

Garrison wasn't very approachable. Which I told him in the next breath.

"I hate your fuckin' face. True story," Garrison growled, shoving me away from him.

I laughed. "You're lying. You love my fuckin' face, which is why you're so upset with me."

Garrison turned on me, and I stopped at the look on his face.

"You being gone scares the shit out of me. I worry constantly whether you'll make it home this time. But I don't complain because I know you fuckin' love it. That doesn't stop the fear in me, though. So how about you stop trying to play it off and for once tell us how you're really feeling," Garrison said accusingly.

I winced.

But they were my brothers, the ones that would have my back no matter what. The ones that did have my back when it mattered most.

"I didn't think I'd make it home this time," I said honestly. "The bomb exploded the minute I stepped foot on the fucking yard that surrounded the motel. Had I not been wearing a bulletproof vest, I would've had shrapnel in my fuckin' heart. I had over ten pieces stuck in my vest."

Silence.

"You did make it home, though. And you're alive and well," Cormac finally said.

I nodded.

It'd been close, though.

I'd thought that I was going to die.

Would have died had Parker not pulled me down with him.

Parker and I, we traded turns saving each other's lives.

Obviously, it was now my turn to do the same for him since he had my back this time.

"I don't want to talk about it anymore. I want to work off some of this aggression," I told them, hastening my steps.

I could practically see the two of them trading off knowing looks, and I hoped that they'd keep their shit comments to themselves.

But they didn't.

"So that's all that's bugging you? You got blown up?" Garrison asked.

I shrugged. "Yeah."

I was lying, and they both knew it.

"Come on, we promise we won't tell," Cormac teased, shoving me forward by planting his foot on my ass and pushing off me.

I turned a glare onto him, but I knew that he liked Thomasina even less than I did.

So I took glee in telling him what I did next.

"I also saw Thomasina today, and she called Ruthie a slut," I blabbed.

"What the fuck did she want?" Cormac growled.

Cormac and Thomasina shared something when we were living together, and I couldn't tell you what. Although I'd asked, he'd refused to tell me, and I'd given him that out.

I picked up the baseball glove and fit it onto my hand.

"Thomasina is the PAR officer. She has the beat that Ruthie's house falls into. And since they've gotten so many complaints on Ruthie from so many different people, Thomasina was sent out to talk to her. Except neither one of us spoke to her because she was so fucking rude," I answered.

"She's still having problems with her neighbors?" Garrison asked, picking up the ball and tossing it up high in the air before catching it once again.

I nodded. "Yeah, I think I'll be staying there for a while...to keep an eye on her and all."

Cormac snorted. "I'm sure that's why you're staying there. All because of her neighbors. I'm sure it has nothing to do with her sweet pus..."

I threw the ball at him, and he caught it with a laugh.

"Touchy, touchy for someone who only wants to protect the girl from the neighbors," Cormac laughed.

I flipped him off.

"I didn't say that was the only reason," I hedged.

"So you *looooooove* her?" Garrison cooed.

I launched the ball at him extra hard, and he caught it with a laugh, pulling his glove off and shaking out his hand.

"You're picking up high school etiquette now, dick wad?" I asked him.

Garrison smiled unrepentantly. "Yeah, that childish crap sure rubs off on you when you're smothered in it every day."

"That's why you don't have a girlfriend," Cormac said.

"You don't have a girlfriend either," Garrison rebuked.

They both looked at me simultaneously.

"Why are you both looking at me?" I asked, picking up the bat and heading for home plate.

Cormac got into position as I adjusted myself into my stance.

The one I always used when I was getting ready to bat.

Left foot planted.

Right foot planted.

Swing three times.

Turn left. Right. Up. Then down.

Finally, I settled my gaze on Cormac and nodded.

Cormac stilled, looked left and right, and then lifted his leg before tossing a fastball at me.

Straight.

Down.

The.

Middle.

I yacked it.

Hit it so hard it sailed over the fence and into the trees beyond the field.

"Boom!" I yelled, running the bases.

It wasn't until I'd run all three bases and hit home plate that I realized neither of my closest cheerers were cheering me on.

"What the fuck?" I asked them.

Garrison was the one to speak.

"You didn't celebrate like a lunatic. What the fuck else is wrong with you?" Garrison asked.

"Just had a bad day," I said, shrugging.

My mind went to the other thing I'd tried very hard not to think about since I'd gotten the news, and I gritted my teeth as I handed the bat off to Cormac and picked up another ball.

"Get ready," I ordered.

Cormac did, but Garrison stayed at my side and stared at me.

"What else? That's not all," Garrison pushed.

Knowing it was futile, that they wouldn't stop until I'd said it all, I finally said what was bothering me the most.

Even more than all of the other stuff.

Last but not least and all that shit.

"And to top it all off, I figured out that my mother is in town…at our old place," I said finally.

Cormac threw the ball at me, and I caught it before turning right around and tossing it at Garrison.

Garrison caught it, firing it right back at Cormac.

Guess he was done batting until we got this all out.

We did this for a long time while nobody spoke.

I thought they'd let it drop, but Garrison finally piped in.

"Why don't you go confront the whore?"

I sighed.

"I have to go back to base in two days. So right now wouldn't be a great time to go. Not to mention I'll be leaving Ruthie here all by herself," I answered.

"You want us to watch over her?" Cormac asked.

I gave him a look.

"And how exactly would you do that from three hours away?" I countered.

He shrugged.

"I can't, but Garrison can," he answered.

Garrison nodded. "I can check on her for you. Let you know if anything else happens to her. I can also talk to the whore for you."

Garrison didn't like my mother.

He was just as annoyed as I was that she'd given me up.

Mostly because he didn't like to see his friends hurt or upset.

He was protective.

He'd taken the role of 'protector' when we'd been in foster care, and hated that he couldn't protect us from all the shit that was thrown at us.

"I can't even think about her right now. I'll explore that when I get home. But you need to keep your nose out of her shit. I better not come back here and find out she knows I'm still here in town," I told the two of them.

Cormac grinned. Garrison scowled.

"We'll see," Garrison finally agreed. "But you won't be going it alone when you do get back. We'll all go together."

"How about we change the subject? Preferably to something that doesn't make me want to puke," I told them.

Cormac smiled.

Garrsion snorted.

"We could talk about the fact that Cormac is going to try out for the Spark's at the end of this month," Garrison supplied.

I froze, ready to throw the ball to Cormac, and asked, "What?"

Cormac glared at Garrison.

"I asked you not to blab about it," Cormac growled.

I blinked. "Why wouldn't you want me to know?"

"I didn't even want this fucker to know," he pointed to Garrison. "I didn't want you to go watch me tryout. Something I know for a fucking fact you'll do now."

I didn't deny it.

We'd gone to every one of Cormac's games that we could, and would continue to do so.

Why?

Because he was our brother.

And I wanted him to be happy.

And baseball made him happy.

"You should try out, too," Cormac offered.

I shot him a look.

"I haven't played in a real game since I was in high school," I told him. "Why would I embarrass myself by going to try out for a professional baseball team?"

"You play games all the time," Cormac defended.

I shook my head. "No I don't. I play recreationally. There's no competition in it. And I have a job. I don't need another one."

Cormac grinned. "You're saying that woman of yours wasn't competition?"

I held my tongue.

Because I knew whatever I said right then would somehow get back to Ruthie.

So I chose my words carefully. "Ruthie's good, don't get me wrong. But she can't throw a hundred mile an hour pitch. Or hit so hard that it'll go out of the park."

"You're just making up excuses for why you're a pussy," Cormac chirped.

I threw the ball at his face, and he caught it easily, firing it right back at me.

I caught it, picked up the bat off the grass, threw it up in the air, and hit it as hard as I could.

Garrison and Cormac both started to run, but they missed it.

It fell just over the top of their heads, having both men cursing.

Dropped balls meant laps had to be run, and I grinned.

"That's right, bitches. Get to running!"

CHAPTER 11

Just got the new DVD: Hot co-ed's try anal 3. Do you think I need to watch the first two to know what's going on?
-Cormac to Sterling

Ruthie

"What's that?" I asked Sterling, pointing to this little stuffed fish on a keychain that looked like it'd been chewed on by a dog, yet Sterling didn't have a dog.

"That's Nemo," he answered as he slipped his shirt on.

"Why does 'Nemo' look like he's been put through a torture device?" I asked.

He shrugged.

"I got it from one of those Adopt A Soldier boxes when I was on my first deployment," he answered, like it was something I should've known.

I looked at him sharply.

It was two days after what I liked to call the 'fiasco,' a.k.a. Sterling going head to head with a police officer.

I still couldn't explain my reaction to it all.

Even now, two days later, I found it extremely sexually frustrating to watch Sterling fight for me.

I think that must've been what I found so arousing about it all.

That he'd actually gone to bat for me, so to speak.

He'd had my back, and he'd been willing to take on a man of the law to make it apparent that he would.

I'd thought he'd been fine about it all when I'd left to go to lunch, and he'd left to go to practice with Cormac.

Something had happened, though.

Something he wasn't willing to talk about, yet.

I'd given him the space, trying to make sure he realized that I wouldn't push if he didn't want me to, but it was getting old.

"So did it come like that, or did it happen after you got it?" I asked, picking the thing up by one barely hanging on fin.

He snatched it out of my hand and shoved the entire thing into his pocket, glaring at me.

"I got it from some kid that said it kept him safe at night when he was younger, and he wanted me to have it since I wasn't going to be safe. I've carried it on every patrol, mission, and flight home since I got it," he explained impatiently.

He was acting like he didn't even want to be here.

And I was getting tired of tiptoeing around him, worried I might cause the beast to wake.

So instead of pushing, I didn't say a word.

I wasn't a confrontational kind of girl.

"Alright," I said, nodding. "I'm gonna go for a run."

I didn't bother to ask him if he wanted to come.

I knew he had to report to the base today, and would most likely be gone when I got home.

But I was terrible at trying to figure out what was wrong with people.

I had enough of my own shit to deal with than to add other's shit to my shit.

"Okay, see you later," he said.

I shook my head and walked to the back door where my shoes were sitting.

I'd changed earlier to running shorts and a tank top, and hadn't planned on running until after he left.

But it bothered me that I cared that he wasn't being very nice, and I didn't want to say anything I'd regret later on.

So my solution was to leave before he could say anything else that would upset me.

I managed to make it outside the back door and into the woods that lined the back of my house in less than thirty seconds.

Except when I passed the fallen tree that was about a hundred yards past my back door, I sat down and stared blindly at the ground beneath my feet.

I hated feeling sad.

And I was definitely feeling sad.

Pathetically so.

I think I was more upset with the fact that Sterling would be gone for two weeks rather than the fact that he wasn't talking to me.

I hadn't realized how much it'd bothered me that he was leaving after everything that'd happened.

He'd only been here for a few days, and he was already leaving.

A tree branch cracked somewhere behind me, and I twisted my back to look behind me, but nobody was there.

Brows furrowing, I got up from my log and started to walk back to my house.

Maybe if I just told him that I understood and that he could talk to me when he was ready, he'd know I was there for him.

He didn't need me acting like a bitch.

He had a lot of things on his plate, and not all of those problems revolved around me.

Except as I arrived back at my house and walked inside, Sterling was gone.

I'd only been gone for ten minutes at most, but he'd left, and I had nobody to blame but myself.

***

"What's your problem?" Lily asked me.

I looked up to find one of my best friends in the world looking at me like she didn't know me.

"Sterling left," I said finally.

There was no point beating around the bush.

I'd told her all about Sterling just a few days ago at my lunch with Sawyer and her.

They knew that I was in love with him.

"Why would he do that? Did y'all have a fight?" She asked worriedly.

I shook my head. "No. He has some sort of training and debriefing. He'll only be gone two weeks…at least that's what he said. But I didn't leave things between us good, and I feel like shit about it."

"What happened?" She questioned, sitting back twirling the fork on top of the table with one finger.

I sighed.

"Well, not much, to be honest. After I got back from lunch with y'all the other day, I came inside and he was just staring at the wall with a blank look on his face," I said. "At first I thought it was just because he was alone, but he kept doing it for the next two days. Then he just sprung the training he had to do for two weeks on me out of the blue, and I was left reeling.

"This morning I was mad at him for not confiding in me what was wrong, so I left to go on a run knowing he was about to leave. And when I turned around to apologize, he was already gone," I told her.

Lily nodded. "I think that an apology on your part will be good, yet I don't see that you did anything wrong here. It seems to me that he just needs to work through his problems on his own, and when he's ready to let you in on what those problems are, he will."

I blinked. "That's all you got?"

She smiled, her straight white teeth were revealed with the brilliance of it.

I couldn't explain how happy seeing her smile like that made me feel.

I loved Lily.

She was my very best friend in the world, and I hadn't seen her smile like that in a very long time.

I was glad she was happy.

"Let me tell you something about *Alphas*," she said, leaning in closer to me.

I snorted, but leaned in, too.

"And what do you have to tell me?" I asked conspiringly.

"Alphas have some sort of switch in their brain that tell them that expressing their feelings is a weakness," she said.

"Oh, this should be good," Lily's husband said, taking a seat beside me and throwing his arm around me. "I've gotta hear this. I might take notes."

Lily ignored her husband, and I leaned into him and rested my head on his shoulder.

Dante Hail was the most awesome guy in the world.

And I'd met some awesome guys before, especially since I'd been in Benton.

He was the owner of a repo business, and defined what one would call 'badass.'

He was tall with blonde hair, chiseled cheekbones, sharp blue eyes, and a friendly smile.

"So by not telling you their feelings, it's not because they don't want you in their business, it's just that they don't know how to express them without looking 'weak.' Something ingrained that makes them feel inadequate in our eyes, so they try not to speak of them," Lily continued.

I smiled at Lily.

She really didn't care that her badass husband was sitting there, listening to her talk about something that was probably a source of constant fights between them.

I'd remembered on many occasions while visiting with Lily during my incarceration how she'd say that her husband was being 'bull headed' and 'stubborn.'

"What are you talking about, Lil?" Dante asked. "You're giving her advice you know nothing about."

"Oh?" She asked. "And how would you suggest she get the information out of him?"

"Honestly?" Dante asked.

Lily nodded

"Ask him. If you want to know, and he wants you to know, he'll tell you. If he doesn't want you to know, he won't tell you. No matter what, though, what he's not telling you doesn't mean he cares about you any less. It just means he's processing it. And when he's ready to tell you, he will," Dante informed us.

I snorted.

That sounded like Sterling.

"So did Lily tell you the good news?" Dante asked jovially.

Lily's eyes went absolutely venomous.

"No," she said through clenched teeth. "I haven't."

I blinked, surprised that she'd taken that tone with her husband.

"What's up?" I asked them, looking in between the two of them like they were something fun and exciting.

Lily finally turned her eyes to me.

"We found out the sex of the baby." she smiled, eyes happy. "And…picked a name."

My stomach clenched.

Again, it wasn't that I wasn't happy for Lily and Dante…it was just that it was hard to hear about other people getting their happily every after's, and I didn't.

What was a gut punch to the stomach was what Lily said next.

"It's another girl, and we've decided to name her Jade Ruthann," she smiled.

"Ohhh," I whispered. "That's beautiful. Congratulations."

What were the odds that she'd choose the name that I was to use all those years ago?

I was surprised I didn't choke on those words.

"I have to use the bathroom. I'll be right back," I whispered, hurrying out of the booth and hurrying to the bathroom.

Lucky for me that I didn't have to go to the public bathroom.

Since we'd decided to have lunch at Halligans and Handcuffs, I was able to slip through the kitchen door and head to the back bathroom without anyone the wiser.

Well…kind of.

I knew Silas saw me.

He saw everything.

His eyes clocked me the moment I walked into the kitchen.

His office was set in the back of the kitchen, and he could see the door from where he was sitting.

He started to stand, but I shook my head at him and practically fell into the bathroom, slamming the door as I went.

I dropped down the toilet lid through tear filled eyes and stared at my hands as I dropped down on top of it.

God, it still hurt so bad.

I could practically feel the way her tiny body had filled my hands.

I'd been able to hold her for hours before they'd finally come for her.

During that time I'd given my police report with her in my hands under the devastated detectives' sympathetic gazes.

I'd dressed her in her tiny newborn outfit that didn't fit her in the slightest.

Wrapped her in the tiny blanket that I'd intended to cover her in as we brought her home from the hospital.

And I'd done it all alone.

Lily and Dante had been half way around the world where Dante had been stationed in Germany in the army.

They'd married a week or two before I'd told Bender that I was pregnant, all because of Dante's orders to be stationed at the Germany base.

I hadn't had contact with her in well over eight months, and I'd been so excited to introduce her to my daughter.

So I knew it wasn't Lily's fault.

She had no clue what was wrong with me.

Had no clue why I'd killed Bender…not really.

She hadn't been able to make it home for the trial, and what little she did know about the entire situation was what I'd told her had happened.

She knew I'd killed Bender in self-defense…what she didn't know was that it'd been because I was in turmoil over him killing my child.

The one piece of me that was good…and pure.

I didn't realize that my sobs had become so gut wrenching until a knock sounded on the door.

"You okay?" A muffled male voice called from the other side.

Silas.

"Yeah," I choked out.

"You don't sound okay," Silas challenged.

"I'm fine," I lied.

I heard something that sounded distinctly similar to 'fucking hardheaded women,' but I couldn't be sure.

"Call me if you need me," Silas ordered.

I nodded, even though he couldn't see me.

"Okay," I said through another sob.

I could practically hear him sigh through the door, and a small smile started to spread on my lips.

I really loved Silas.

I loved him for Sawyer.

Loved that he treated my good friend with the tenderness that she deserved.

I didn't like that he was putting his nose into my business.

I craved independence like crops need rain.

I'd become so accustomed to doing what I was told to do, that sometimes I didn't even realize I was following orders until I'd already followed them and couldn't unfollow them.

However, these men…these Dixie Wardens…they gave me the independence that I craved, and always watched over me.

Something Sterling had said would happen.

'We look out for our own…and baby, you're mine.'

That'd come out of Sterling's mouth the night before as we'd been lying in bed discussing the politics of motorcycle clubs.

I let my head fall back as I thought about all that I had to think about.

I'd made the decision to move out of my rental, and the couple I'd rented from had already agreed to let me rent another place that was about ten minutes from town.

Something I'd been intending to tell Sterling, seeing as I was supposed to be moved out by the end of the week.

I'd also gotten Dane, with his huge car hauler, to help me move.

Tonight, after I got home from my lunch with Lily, I'd start packing boxes I'd gotten from the local super market.

Then when I was ready, I'd be moving to the new house.

Although the only one I could get on this short of notice and not break my lease was one just a street over from the one I was at now.

A new set of neighbors would mean less problems...hopefully.

With quick thinking, I texted Lily that I was going home on account of I forgot about a pest control appointment, unlocked the bathroom door, and then eyed the window in the corner of the bathroom.

It was directly behind the toilet, so I used the metal trashcan beside the toilet to stand on, and unlocked the window.

It slid open easily, and luckily it had a large enough ledge to allow me to straddle the opening, allowing me to not fall, and instead slide out rather gracefully.

I landed on the concrete besides the building with nearly silent feet, and then turned to close the window.

Once I had it closed, I turned and started walking towards my car, ignoring the group of men that'd gathered outside the bar as I did.

It was Friday night, so it didn't surprise me in the least that there was already a line waiting to get in the door.

What did surprise me though was the graceful older couple standing a little further away from the man.

They didn't look the type to go into a bar to eat...not with those clothes anyway.

And they really weren't dressed for a bar.

The woman wore white linen pants, a pale lavender silk shirt, and a scarf around her delicate neck.

She had dirty blonde hair that was styled in long, loose waves down her back.

And although she looked familiar, it was the man at her side that held my attention.

He was tall.

Really tall.

He was older, but not really old.

He had blonde hair with a hint of red in it when he moved, and sharp gray eyes that took in everything around him without actually moving an inch.

He was wearing a similar dressy outfit to the woman at his side, but he was wearing black slacks and a pale lavender button down shirt.

His eyes caught me as I looked at him, and they narrowed, marking my turn to leave with haste.

I couldn't figure out what it was about that man that had me staring at him so, but I knew it wouldn't solve anything to keep staring.

And if I didn't hurry, then Silas would realize I wasn't in the bathroom anymore and come looking for me.

He felt some sort of responsibility for me, and I hated that.

So, in my haste to get out of there, I didn't realize that the man I'd been watching was now watching me in turn.

I didn't see how his face turned down in a frown.

Nor the way he pulled out his wallet and looked at a picture from a long ago time.

Because had I seen that, I wouldn't have been so surprised just a few days later when Sterling came home.

CHAPTER 12

Do you ever start crying about something that's weak, and realize the next day when you get your period that you weren't a weak ass bitch after all?
-E-Card

Ruthie

My eyes stared blankly at the TV screen.

I was watching the ten o'clock news and thinking about how shitty a day it'd been.

Tips had been shit.

Customers had been even more shit.

At least Silas hadn't caught on, or it could've been even worse.

Any time he caught on, my measly tips suffered even more.

"An Amber Alert has been issued for an eleven month old baby that was stolen from a gas station this morning by the child's mother, who is thought to be unstable. The child was in his father's car while he was pumping gas, and while he was busy at the pump, he didn't realize that his child was being taken from the backseat," the news anchor droned.

I looked up, seeing a grainy picture of a woman with brown hair taking the young child out of the car while the man looked in the other direction. He never even realized it'd happened. Drove off and left without a second thought.

Something that I was sure every parent wouldn't think to check.

Then a picture of the child was displayed on the screen, and I smiled sadly at the man and the child.

The man was holding the child against his chest, the boy clutching a plastic dump truck in both hands that was bigger than his body.

They looked happy.

And it broke my heart that this would happen to him.

"Baby Donnie has a distinctive birth mark on the left side of his neck in the shape of a heart. If you see him, alert authorities immediately, but do not approach the woman. She is suspected to be armed and volatile," the news anchor said animatedly.

I turned off the TV with a flick of my wrist, taking a look around at my now packed up rental house.

The only thing that was left out of the boxes were the sheets on my bed, the clothes I'd be wearing tomorrow, and my TV.

Everything else was packed and ready to go.

I looked down at my phone on the couch in front of me and willed it to ring.

It'd been four days now without any contact from Sterling whatsoever.

Not even an 'I arrived okay.'

Zero. Zilch. Nada. *Nothing*.

Leaving my phone on my couch in hopes that I wouldn't check it thirty times before I laid my head down for the night, I walked into the bedroom and flopped down into bed, completely exhausted.

My eyes got heavy, but that still didn't stop my mind from wandering where I didn't want it to be.

But it seemed a certain man with green eyes and dirty blonde hair had a way at keeping me on his mind…even in my dreams.

***

Three hours later, I woke up to my last day in my house with it on fire.

Smoke was billowing into my small bedroom, but with my bedroom door, it only had a limited place to come in.

But as I said that, the door slammed open and an imposing figure in a yellow jacket started through the doorway.

Smoke poured through even faster behind the figure, and soon it became harder to breathe.

"Shit," I said, dropping down onto the floor on my hands and knees.

"Ruthie!" Darth Vader called.

I looked up to see the yellow jacketed man about three inches from my face, and realized that I was disoriented.

"Ruthie!" Darth said again.

I blinked.

"Yes, Darth?" I asked, somewhat delusional from oxygen deprivation.

The yellow-jacketed man moved his mask aside and placed it over my face, allowing me a few blissful mouthfuls of oxygen before he removed the mask again.

"It's me," the man said.

It took me a few minutes before I realized just who 'me' was, and then I smiled, launching myself at him.

"Zander!" I cried, so happy to see the goofball that I didn't contemplate what I did next.

I threw myself in his arms, hugging him so tightly around the neck that he choked out a, "you're okay."

"Thank you so much for coming for me!" I gasped.

He patted my back and started to crawl.

Inevitably, I ended up on the floor beside him, my hand in his as we crawled together.

I couldn't see a damn thing with all the smoke, and the moment we made it to what, I guessed, used to be the living room, I was praying that it wouldn't be much further.

And it wasn't.

Only a few short crawls more, and I felt the familiar feeling of a doorway.

Zander pushed me through it, and I fell face first into a man's ass.

A man I hadn't realized was in front of me until I became acquainted with his butt.

"Ack," I exclaimed.

The man didn't budge when I hit him, even when I sprawled ungracefully against his backside.

Then my hands were grabbed and I was hauled off my front porch before I was unceremoniously dumped on my front lawn.

"Ruthie!" Zander said, patting my face.

Except I couldn't look at him.

I was too busy looking at my house burning.

All of my things that I'd managed to gather over the last seven months were gone.

Every. Last. One of them.

Then a thought occurred to me, and I was up and running back towards the front door before anybody could stop me.

I didn't have to get far, though.

All I had to do was make it back up to the front porch, right inside the door.

I held my breath until I was dizzy, feeling around for the familiar hook that I hung all my bags from that I needed for the next day.

And as soon as my hand closed around it and I lifted it off the hook, strong arms encircled my ribcage and I was yanked back so hard that my head snapped.

I gasped in a full lungful of smoke filled air, and started to gag.

Then I started to cough as I was dragged further and further away from my home.

"Why'd you go back into the building?" Sterling yelled as he shook me, fuming.

I held out my hand, offering him the book in my hands, and his face completely fell.

"Fuck," he sighed. "Just *fuck*."

I nodded.

It was Jade's baby book.

It had her tiny footprints…and her tiny handprints. A lock of her dark brown hair, and a few dozen pictures of her that the nurse had been kind enough to take for me.

"I couldn't leave her behind," I whispered brokenly.

His eyes closed, and he leaned his head forward until it rested on my shoulder.

"You could've died," he whispered.

I didn't know what to say to that.

I could have.

I didn't want to lie. He'd know I was lying…so it defeated the purpose.

"Yo!" A voice barked, interrupting our little bubble.

I blinked, finally looking around the area.

I was at the curb now instead of on my front lawn, which was good since I could clearly see that the house was fully engulfed now.

Firemen worked hurriedly around us, massive fire hoses snaking along from the road beyond my driveway.

People surrounded a makeshift barrier of fire trucks and police cruisers.

Two bikes were parked haphazardly in the middle of it all.

One of which I knew to be Sterling's, and the other one I'd never seen before.

"She needs to put on this mask," a medic ordered from beside me.

I didn't look away from the bikes.

Only kept staring as I thought about all that had happened in the last ten minutes.

It felt like hours.

"Y'all need to back up so my men can work," Sebastian ordered, pointing to a point where there were more men standing around.

"Go over there. Stay with the cop who's standing beside her cruiser," Sterling ordered.

My eyes followed where he was pointing, coming to the conclusion that Sterling wouldn't be following me over there, otherwise he would've led me to her.

"What are you doing here?" I asked softly.

His eyes connected with mine, and became somewhat softer.

"We'll talk…just not right now. Go over there and be good," he ordered once again.

I sighed and let go of his hand, walking away from him.

His stare stayed on my back as I moved through the crowd of people, coming to a stop next to a woman police officer who looked like she'd rather be anywhere else but here.

"How are you doing?" She asked reluctantly.

I smiled. "I'm fine, thanks."

"No, she'd be better if she put this oxygen mask on her face," the same persistent paramedic sniped from my side.

I sighed and turned, holding my hand out.

"Give it to me," I snapped.

The medic gave me the facemask and I placed it over my nose and mouth, annoyed that she was making me wear it when I felt perfectly fine.

Except when she started the oxygen, I immediately realized how much easier it was to breathe, and inadvertently let out a small sigh of relief.

"Good," the medic said. "Keep this on. I'll come check on you after I check on the firefighter."

I blinked, turning to find Zander sitting on the back of the medic, his eyes focused on me…or at least my area.

When I moved, his eyes didn't even flicker.

And then I realized it wasn't me he was watching, but the police officer at my side.

"You've got an admirer," I said through my mask.

The officer looked down.

"What?" She asked.

I lifted my mask and said, "You've got an admirer."

She looked over at the fire truck, and I was impressed with how she knew exactly whom I was talking about without asking.

"Yeah, he's an...ex," she said.

My brows rose.

What'd they do, graduate high school together?

Were they high school sweethearts?

"He looks into you," I observed, watching how they watched each other.

Zander moved his big body so that the medic who was in front of him was more to his left, freeing up the area directly in front of him for his viewing pleasure.

"Well...he's not into the fact that I'm a cop...so he can't be *that* into me," she finally offered.

I blinked, surprised that she'd admit that.

All the female cops I'd met over my time didn't like to share feelings, and either this woman at my side didn't mind sharing her feelings, or she was tired of holding those feelings in.

My bet was on the latter.

"How long did y'all date?" I asked, eyes scanning the area for the only man that would ever be on my mind.

"He's by the fire truck on the right side," she said. "And we dated for six years, all the way through high school and the first two years of college. We've been separated for two years now."

And they still had it this bad.

Imagine that.

I turned my head to find the man that currently meant the whole world to me and found him exactly where the young cop at my side said I would.

He was talking to some man I'd never met before, Sebastian, and Torren.

Sterling had his hands resting on top of his head, as if he was so relived he could barely contain it.

He must've sensed my gaze, because he turned and offered me a wink.

I waved back, but the order of the cop at my side was what had me jumping.

"Put your oxygen back on before he comes over here," she ordered quickly.

I quickly complied, looking over at Zander with the now finished paramedic staring at me in anger.

"She's a strict woman," I said.

"She's the reason we broke up," the cop confided.

"Why?" I asked.

Was it weird that I was having this conversation with a practical stranger?

Because I thought maybe it was.

But it was taking my mind off the matter of someone burning my house down.

Because I didn't doubt for one freakin' minute that this wasn't deliberate.

I'm sure they wouldn't have gone to such exuberant measures had they known I was planning on moving anyway.

But now it was somewhat comical, since I knew for a fact that there were cameras on the house…something I imagined Sterling was discussing with the police officer on his right, and Sebastian that was on his left.

He hadn't specifically told me he had a camera on my house, but it was kind of obvious when I saw new wires leading into a battery pack in one closet.

Well, I'd had to Google it…but I'd figured it out eventually.

"I think they're in love with each other," the cop continued.

"How did you realize they were in love?" I asked.

"They're partners. She calls…texts…invites him out. He was sacrificing time with me on his days off to spend time with her…even though he'd just had a whole day with her and not with me," she continued.

I didn't know what to say to that.

That did sound bad.

"Looks like he still likes you," I said finally, not sure what she was looking for here.

"Nothing you can say. Thank you for listening to me," she said.

Her radio squawked, and she moved to the side to speak into it privately.

"It's trash like you who ruined this street," a woman at my side sneered.

I looked over at the woman who'd just spewed that venom, and couldn't help the tear that slipped out of the corner of my eye.

"What did I do to deserve your hostility?" I asked woodenly.

She sneered, her son in her arms as he slept away, blissfully unaware.

"You brought this trash to our neighborhood…you know it was because of you," she pointed at me.

The movement woke the child in her arms enough that he switched sides of his face of which he was laying on, and it was then I saw the mark on his neck.

A perfect heart shaped birth mark that was plain as day, even under the harsh glow of emergency lights that lit up the night.

I'd seen that birthmark on the news earlier.

In fact, I remembered thinking to myself how good it was that he such an identifying mark because if anyone did spot the child, he'd be recognized almost immediately.

I didn't know what to do.

I vaguely remembered the news anchor saying that she was volatile, and might have weapons.

Yet, I didn't want to leave her here with the kid.

What if she ran off?

So what did I do?

Did what I did best…piss off my neighbors.

"Why do you care? Just go back inside your house and close the door. No harm no foul," I sniped.

"I can't go back inside my house, the firefighters made us evacuate due to your piece of shit house being on fire," she hissed.

The child blinked sleepily at me, and it was then I saw that the child was exhausted.

He had dark circles underneath his eyes, and they were red rimmed from what looked to be hours of crying.

Everybody knew what that looked like…because most people did it at least once in their life.

The kind of crying where you can't stop, because you see no way out.

"Are you the bitch who's been calling the cops on me because of my car being in the road?" I asked her.

She narrowed her eyes.

"No, but had I, you would've deserved it. We don't need your kind of trash in this neighborhood. This is a family neighborhood, not a murdering one," she snapped. "It's probably a good thing that your house is gone. Saves me the trouble."

The last comment was said in such low tones, that I wasn't sure it was meant to be heard.

But I had.

And so had Sterling who'd come up behind her.

He opened his mouth to speak, and I shook my head hard at him.

The woman kept her eyes averted from me, completely dismissing me, and I was never more thankful.

Mostly because I started to do some weird sign language at Sterling, who had no freakin' idea what I was talking about.

His brow furrowed, and when I widened my eyes and flared them at the woman, he looked in the direction of her, then turned back to me with a 'what the fuck?' face.

I sighed.

Men were so freakin' stupid!

How hard was it to understand a cutting throat signal and a point at the woman?

I mean, wouldn't you at least assume she was some sort of killer…at the scene of a freakin' fire?

Sure, she may not be the actual one who set the house on fire, but in a pinch, I'd work with it.

Because the execution of it all would still be the same.

The woman would get taken into custody, and that child would be taken away from her.

End goals, people! End goals!

I finally resorted to walking over to him, getting up on tiptoes, and whispering in his ear.

"Saw the news earlier. This woman kidnapped that child in her arms," I said as softly as I could.

He squeezed my ass to let me know he understood, and turned, catching the eye of Trance who was now standing in the circle he'd been in earlier.

Then like freakin' magic, he did a series of hand signals that looked nothing like mine, and Trance nodded in understanding, breaking off from the group with his K-9 unit, Kosher, and started our way.

He caught two other officers on the way, again with the hand signals, and surrounded the woman before she could even protest.

My mouth dropped open as they had the child out of her arms, and cuffs on her hands in less than thirty seconds.

"Holy cow," I whispered in awe. "You're hand signals are *way* better."

"That's because I was using hand signals and not made up shit that doesn't do anyone any good," Sterling muttered.

Okay, he was still pissy.

Dually noted.

"I'm going to get the officer," he gestured to the woman officer I'd been speaking with earlier. "To take you to a hotel. If I can find time, I'll stop by…but this may take all night."

I nodded. "Okay."

What else was there to say?

Nothing he needed to hear right then.

I knew he was worried about me…about my situation.

And I didn't want to be that woman that threw a hissy fit because she wanted a freakin' hug from her boyfriend. One that wasn't out of anger because she'd gone into a burning building for something that didn't matter more than her life.

Something I'd done…and probably shouldn't have.

Would I do it again?

Yes.

But I hated that he was there to witness it.

"Don't do anything stupid. Don't order room service, don't call anyone on the phone. Wait for me to get there. Promise," he said briskly.

He didn't deserve to have another worry added onto his plate.

Something I knew for a fact that he did.

Constantly.

He was a worrywart.

Which was also why I knew he'd overthink everything to death before he actually put any plans into action.

"Okay, Sterling."

He nodded and turned on his heel, walking back to Sebastian and now that I looked closer, Silas.

Once he arrived back at the huddle, and intense conversation ensued.

And I was left chanting to myself.

Don't cry. Don't cry.

I didn't cry.

At least not until I got to my hotel room, that was.

There I broke down.

There I cried for my lost things.

My only possessions in life.

The worry that I kept putting on Sterling and my friends.

Maybe…maybe it was time for me to leave.

Maybe that would be best for everyone.

I couldn't say that my mind was in the best place…but the next morning, I had my answer. It was time to go.

CHAPTER 13

I hate you more than I love chocolate.
-Ruthie's secret thoughts

Ruthie

"I'm sorry, Ms. Comalsky, but I can't risk anymore of my properties. You'll have your deposit returned as of Monday morning, and I'll be waiving your contract," Carol, the woman I was renting the property from, said.

Tears stung my eyes as what I'd feared would happen, happened.

I opened my eyes as a sob tore out of my mouth.

"It's okay," I said. "Thank you for calling."

Without waiting for her to continue, I pressed the red 'end call' button.

Then turned the whole thing off completely.

The new phone that'd been delivered to me about twenty minutes before hadn't stopped ringing since I'd gotten it.

This one was much nicer than the one that burned up in the fire.

And I knew that Sterling was responsible for getting it, as well as the ten bags of clothes.

I just wished he'd been the one to deliver them instead of the biker prospect...something he'd called himself that I was extremely interested in understanding what it meant. But not in the right state of mind to handle a full-blown conversation about biker business and hierarchy.

With single-minded determination, I walked out of the hotel room with only the phone and one set of clothes I'd gotten out of the bag.

The cheapest thing in the entire bundle.

Sterling hadn't skimped.

Or whoever had purchased the clothes on Sterling's behalf hadn't skimped.

It was all very expensive…or much more expensive than my Wal-Mart tastes.

With the door opened, I was unsurprised to find that there was a biker prospect sleeping against the outside wall.

He'd get reamed later for sleeping and letting me out of my room, but that wasn't my problem.

Right now, what my problem was, was that nobody wanted me here, and my mind wasn't in the right place to stay.

So, closing the door to my hotel room quietly, I headed in the opposite direction of the elevator since I knew it was loud and would probably wake up Mr. Biker Prospect.

Instead I took the stairs, and about had a freak out when I saw the wall of leather that was half way up the stairs I was about to go down.

I didn't know him, though, and I was glad.

"Hi," I said, passing him.

"Hi," he muttered.

I didn't wait to see what he did as I passed, only hurried down the three flights of stairs to the very bottom floor.

After scanning the lobby behind the closed stairwell door, I hurried out and took the exit at the side that would spit me out by the pool.

Something I'd noticed this morning…or last night.

Hell, I didn't even know what time it was.

I skirted around twelve kids who were playing around the open area in front of the pool, threading in and out of the lounge chairs covered in colorful beach towels.

"Hey," one of the mother's on the lounge chairs said. "Did you hear about that baby being found?"

Another woman on the next lounge over made an affirmative noise. "Mmm-hmm," she said, not opening her eyes. "Some lady found him at the scene of a fire. Wonder what happened."

You don't want to know what happened, because my life is depressing and is bound to put anyone in a horrible mood.

I kept walking, not making eye contact with any of them.

I finally came to a stop at the side gate and lifted up the latch that would allow me to exit out into the parking lot.

This was a really nice hotel, and yet another thing Sterling had to cover for me.

I didn't have any cash or credit cards…only managing to grab the one bag that had nothing in it but my most important documents.

Although I was happy to have those, and would need them to access my driver's license and bank accounts, it would've also been smart of me to grab my purse that was on the same damn hook.

"Watch your step," a man said in front of me.

I looked up and smiled at the man.

He was wearing a black polo and jeans, and on the black polo it denoted him as a member of KPD SWAT.

"Thanks," I said, stepping down off the curb.

"No problem," he muttered.

I kept walking until I arrived at the bus stop that I'd spied last night, then took a seat.

My car had been totaled right along with my house, and with only liability insurance on it, I wouldn't be getting a new one anytime soon.

I watched as car after car drove by, so lost in thought that I didn't realize some man had stopped his car in front of me until he finally yelled.

"You need a ride?" He asked.

I blinked.

The man looked familiar.

Very familiar.

"No thanks," I said automatically.

Then with a shake of his head, he left, and I was left to contemplate the cars once again.

I wondered how long it would take the bus to get here.

Couple of hours? Twenty minutes?

I was in Shreveport; surely the bus ran constantly.

Then the bench shifted as someone sat, and I looked over to see the man who'd stopped his car in front of me earlier.

"I saw you at that club, Halligans and Handcuffs, the other night," the man started.

I nodded. "I saw you, too."

And I still thought about the man, even a week later.

There was just something about him that had me curious.

He reminded me of someone from my past, but I couldn't quite tell who he reminded me of.

"So I did some research and found out you worked there," he said.

I nodded.

Did work there. In the past tense.

Not that he'd know that.

I also couldn't figure out why it didn't freak me out that this man had stopped to talk to me, and had looked into me.

I just knew that he was a good man.

A nosy one…but a good one nonetheless.

"Okay…" I said.

My bus chose that minute to pull up, and I stood. "Well, I gotta go. It was nice talking to you."

However, I dropped right back down on my ass the moment the next words came out of his mouth.

"And I realized that you were who I'd been looking for fifteen years," he said. "My daughter."

***

My father looked down at the cell phone that hadn't stopped ringing in over thirty minutes.

"You gonna get that?" He finally asked.

I shook my head.

I'd turned it on to look the man, Able Spiers, up.

He was an oil man who was worth tens of millions of dollars, if not *more.*

And I'd grown up dirt poor.

I'd gone to college on student loans...and amazingly still had them even though I'd been on the inside for years.

I ignored Sterling's phone calls.

"Can you say that again?" I asked.

I was sitting at a table in Cracker Barrel, stunned beyond belief.

The man in front of me with his strawberry blonde hair, and gray eyes just like mine, was the man I'd been hoping for since I was a young kid.

A man that never showed when I needed him.

A man that I used to lay in bed at night and think about saving me from the monsters of my past and present.

"I have a trust fund for you...it's something I've been putting into an account for you since I knew you were mine," the man said.

I ignored the 'trust fund' part of his statement for the more important part.

"You knew I was yours? How?" I asked sharply.

And if he'd known...why didn't he look for me? Why was I left to suffer in a foster home with parents that didn't want me?

"Your mother. She told me about you, and then gave me a sob story about how you were scared of your own shadow, and that I should get to know you first, let you trust me before we told you that you were mine," he answered.

"Listen, Able," I said. "I don't know what you think is happening here, but it doesn't inspire hearts and flowers in my soul to know that you knew about me but didn't try any harder to find me."

"I tried for the last fifteen years, darlin.' I just couldn't find you. Your mother…whatever the fuck happened to her…was dead, and nobody knew where you were. All your mother's neighbors never even knew she had a kid," Able said.

I rolled my eyes.

My mom was a whore at the best of times. And having a kid cramped her style.

She didn't like people knowing she had a kid.

'Kids ruin your pussy,' she'd say. *'Gotta make them think that you're not here.'*

Which was also why I never got toys, and rarely ever went out during the light of day.

Something I still remember vividly to this day.

When I started school, once I was abandoned, I was very behind on my learning. So behind that I had to start school in the third grade instead of the fifth.

But I worked my ass off to get back on track, something that I got complimented on quite a lot when I was trying to get back to my grade.

I even managed to graduate six months early, which, for me, was quite impressive.

Guess anyone could do wonders if they're let out of their house.

"That's true," I amended. "My mother didn't like letting people know I was alive."

I didn't want to ask why my father had known my mother in the first place.

It was bad enough to know that someone like this man slept with someone like my mother.

Had she trapped him? Forced him? Blackmailed him?

The list of possibilities was endless, and I hated that my 'father' had fallen for my mother's shit…just like man after man had fallen.

My mother was what you'd call a 'manipulative bitch.'

She was good.

So good.

She knew how to act to get the maximum attention from *any* man.

She could walk into a bar and instantly know which man was the richest in the room, and after studying him for only minutes, know exactly what to do to get him to latch onto her.

Whether she needed to weave a sob story…or come on strong. Whether she needed to bitch about her abusive husband to get the man's protective instincts turned on full force.

You name it and she could accomplish that persona.

And it was sickening.

Something I could watch my mother accomplish even at the young age of ten years old.

I wasn't a stupid girl by any means, and I knew exactly what my mother was doing.

Which was why I always…always…told the truth, even if it hurt.

Which was also why, that day when cops had come to answer the 911 call I'd made, I'd told them I was of sane mind. I hadn't said a thing to defend myself.

Because I wasn't insane with grief.

I knew exactly what was happening, and was of sound mind and body as I shot my husband.

"So after I started to search for you, I seemed to hit dead end after dead end. Checked hospitals and police stations. Put your face onto a milk carton," he answered. "You were just *gone*."

My mother dropped me off at a hospital. She'd gone outside to grab her wallet while I was getting screened for a concussion that I never had, and just never came back.

It was a hospital in a small town that I'd never heard of before, at least when I was a child, and the search for my mother didn't last long.

Apparently, it was something that happened a lot...usually only with younger kids...not ten year olds.

"I'm sorry," I told him honestly.

My mother had been a shit head...what could I say?

I'd done my best not to become her.

Had gone to classes.

Gone to college.

Had a life...at least until Bender came along.

"Not your doing, honey girl. Just wish I would've seen you a long time ago. Although you're a long way from El Paso, Texas," he answered.

I nodded.

It was weird how things worked.

Lily and I had decided to go all the way to the University of Louisiana in Monroe, Louisiana of all places once we graduated high school.

Bender was the only one from our high school that was going there, on a scholarship. That didn't really enter into our decision. I'm not even sure we knew that he was going to be around that area. We just wanted out.

We'd chosen a place on the map that was close enough to get to with one bus ticket, and was a good school to boot.

It worked out for Lily...*just not for me.*

"Doesn't mean I don't feel somewhat responsible. I knew my mom's information. I could've told them what it was...I just didn't want to. I didn't want to be associated with her anymore. I hated her...hated how I wasn't allowed to go outside. Hated how she kept me in a closet when she had her men over. Hated how she 'forgot' to feed me. Hated how I had to listen to her and her conquests have sex all night long. Hated that I had such a drive to learn...yet she wouldn't let me. I hated her. Hated my life. I wanted something different...so I just didn't tell them who I was. Had I done that," I shook my head. "I could've had a different life."

"But you wouldn't have *me*," an achingly familiar voice said from behind me.

I closed my eyes as Sterling's deep baritone voice slid over me, filling me up in places that I hadn't realized were empty. The man had the power to bring me to my knees, yet he never once asked that of me. He loved me...and I was glad he'd come looking. I hadn't wanted to leave...only needed a reason to stay. Needed him to put forth the effort. Because I wouldn't turn out to be my mother. Wouldn't live off of any man that I'd manipulated into keeping me with him.

I didn't turn around, but my eyes closed in happiness when Sterling's hands started to tangle in my hair.

"Why are you here?" He asked.

I could tell that was directed at Able without even looking to clarify.

Able was shooting death rays at Sterling over my head, and I wanted to smile at how 'dad like' it was.

But then the tension started to slowly make itself known, and I froze in my seat as I took stock of what was going on.

How Sterling's hand in my hair had come to a standstill.

How Able looked at Sterling like he was the scum of the earth.

"What's going on?" I finally asked, worried.

"How about you tell me why you're having breakfast with my stepfather when you should be waiting for me at the hotel room I paid for," Sterling snapped.

CHAPTER 14

I suck at apologies. So unfuck you…or whatever
-Ruthie to Sterling

Sterling

"Thanks," I muttered, walking inside the restaurant and walking straight past the hostess stand.

"Sir, can I help…"

I held up my hand to the woman and kept walking, heading straight to the woman that had left without so much as a word.

Who would've left me had she not been stopped.

By the man I'd had under surveillance since I'd come home from that clusterfuck of a mission.

I'd been talking to Loki about the man we saw set fire to Ruthie's house when I'd received a call from the prospect saying he couldn't find Ruthie. Then another, not even twenty minutes later, saying that the man I was watching, Able, had picked up whom he thought was my woman.

And when I'd come to the restaurant that the prospect, Alfie, had followed them to, I'd seen the two of them in a deep conversation.

Which led me to now as I stalked into the building and headed to the table I'd seen her sitting at through the window.

She was in the exact same spot, only I couldn't see her face.

Able saw mine, though, and stiffened.

Ruthie didn't, though.

She kept talking animatedly, moving her hands and body as she spoke.

"Doesn't mean I don't feel somewhat responsible. I knew my mom's information. I could've told them what it was…I just didn't want to. I didn't want to be associated with her anymore. I hated her…hated how I wasn't allowed to go outside. Hated how she kept me in a closet when she had her men over. Hated how she 'forgot' to feed me. Hated how I had to listen to her and her conquests have sex all night long. Hated that I had such a drive to learn…yet she wouldn't let me. I hated her. Hated my life. I wanted something different…so I just didn't tell them who I was. Had I done that," I shook my head. "I could've had a different life."

"*But you wouldn't have me*," I whispered darkly from behind her.

She shivered, and my heart leapt at seeing the way she reacted to my voice.

"Why are you here?" I asked Able, moving forward to tangle my hand in Ruthie's hair.

His jaw clenched as he glared at me.

He didn't want to talk to me.

He knew me, as I knew him.

Knew I was his wife's son.

Something he wouldn't want to tell Ruthie, but I had a feeling he knew.

Knew I was with Ruthie, and didn't like it.

When I read the knowledge in his eyes, I smiled at him.

"How about you tell me why you're having breakfast with my stepfather when you should be waiting for me at the hotel room I paid for," I said, tightening my hand in her hair and pulling her head back to look at me.

She blinked.

"You never came home," she accused.

I let her hair go when she stood and turned to me.

"That was because I was trying to find the man who lit your house on fire!" I growled. "Why are you here with him?"

"Why didn't you let me go to your place?" She countered.

I blinked. "Because I don't have a place."

"You don't have a place...for real?" She asked.

I shook my head. "Normally, I just stay at Garrison's, and I couldn't get ahold of him. When I couldn't get ahold of him, I did the only thing I could and took you to a hotel."

She instantly slumped. "Well how the hell have I not known that before?"

I shook my head. "I don't know. Guess it never came up."

She closed her eyes and leaned her head forward, but the man at her back stood and glared daggers at me.

"Why do you have your hands on my daughter?" He asked.

I stilled, hand tightening on my arm that was around Ruthie's body.

"Daughter?" I asked, feigning ignorance.

Ruthie leaned back. "Yeah...so I found out he's my father."

"What I'd like to know is why you have your hands around her...especially if, in all technicality, she's your sister," Able said.

Out of all the words that could've come out of the piece of shit's mouth, 'sister' hadn't been one that I was expecting.

Denial, yes.

Hatred, yes.

Incest accusations, no.

"She's not my sister," I said forcefully.

"She's my daughter and I'm married to your mother. That makes you family," Able contradicted.

I felt Ruthie stiffen, then look up at me in concern.

"No, that makes it a coincidence. Especially since we haven't seen you all in a very long time. Hell, I didn't even know my mother was still alive until a few days ago when my president told me she was back in town," I told him. "And I met Ruthie over nine months ago."

Able ground his teeth and I could tell he wanted to say something to the contrary.

But as soon as I'd found out about him and my mother being in town, I'd had Silas start looking into why the two of them were here since she'd dropped me off and forced me to leave her.

Why she'd, all of a sudden, popped up out of nowhere. Why now?

But I hadn't been able to figure out why they were here.

So I'd just had them followed.

Done some research on Able Spiers.

"Sterling," Ruthie said, not loosening her hold on me, even after the revelation. "What the hell's going on?"

I shook my head. "I don't know, baby. I think it's time for your *father* to talk."

"You're married to his mother?" Ruthie asked a little bit loudly.

Which garnered the attention of the patrons surrounding us.

"Sit down," Able ordered. "And try not to talk too loud."

Ruthie looked to me, and I nodded, helping her back into her chair before taking the one beside her.

It made me happy that she'd deferred to me.

That she looked to me before the man in front of her that very well could be her father, although it'd yet to be determined.

"Talk," I demanded. "How'd you find her? Why'd you come here?"

Able's eyes narrowed and his jaw clenched.

He didn't look to be the type to take orders.

"Your mother doesn't realize that you're here. She thinks you're still in the Navy, as happy as could be," Able started.

My brows rose. "Really? But I *am* in the Navy. And I am *happy*."

He waved his hand in the air. "I know that. She thinks you're stationed in California."

"Why would she think that?" I asked, anger bristling my words.

"Because I told her."

"Why?"

That came from Ruthie.

Always the protector.

"Because it hurts her to know that her son won't talk to her."

"She wrote you constantly. So much that her fingers bled. She sent you a note every day for ten years…until I asked her to stop," Able said.

"Why would you do that?" I asked. "And why didn't I get any of these letters?"

He shook his head. "I just figured you were being a little fucker. Which was why I protected her…now I can see that maybe I was mistaken."

My brows rose. "And you didn't think to say…talk to me?"

His eyes narrowed. "I had tabs being kept on you. Knew you were okay."

I laughed humorlessly, and Ruthie wrapped her small arms around me from the side, pulling me into her and hugging me as tightly as she could.

She probably knew that I was going to fucking detonate.

She knew that it was a sore subject.

It'd already caused a lot of problems between the two of us.

She'd accused me of never telling her anything.

In all honesty, I didn't like talking about some things.

But what I most hated talking about was my mother.

I'd loved the woman to death, yet that woman hadn't actively tried to search for me…which was why it didn't matter that she'd written me letters.

I was a fuckin' kid when she abandoned me.

I knew, that on some level, she thought she was doing the right thing.

And from an adult's prospective, thinking about the fact that I was an abused child and she couldn't protect me, it made sense.

It didn't make it hurt any less, but it still made sense.

But that didn't matter right now.

What mattered was that my woman's father was in front of her, and she was probably feeling a lot like I'd felt when I heard my mother was in town.

Betrayed and a little bit sad.

"Okay, that still doesn't explain why you're here, talking to her," I continued.

He nodded. "I saw her picture in the paper. Your mother likes to keep up with the happenings from 'home,' so we get the Benton Chronicle sent to us in the mail. It was there I saw the article on her and her job at the gas station."

I nodded. "Okay. So you what, saw her and felt that you needed to come up here urgently?"

His eyes narrowed. "I saw her photo standing next to the older man and knew in my heart that it was her. My kid. So I sent some investigators to find out everything they could about you."

There'd been a picture in the newspaper with Mr. Adam's in front of Dane's Stop and Go. It'd been in celebration of Mr. Adam's massive catfish that he managed to catch.

It'd been a new state record, and he'd attributed his win to Ruthie and her coffee.

Something that Ruthie thought was hilarious.

"And you found me?" I asked.

"Yeah," he nodded. "I did. Found that you were dating her…and I had to let her know she was making a mistake."

"Sterling's a part of my life. Let's just get that straight now. If you don't like it, then you're going to need to back off," Ruthie said softly. "Because I'm not ever giving him up. He was there when nobody else was. There's nothing you can say or do to change my feelings for him."

My heart felt full as she declared that, and smiled at her.

Then Able rocked our worlds.

"Your little brother and sister won't understand that their brother and sister are together."

We both froze.

So we had a brother and sister?

What the fuck was that about?

I could tell Ruthie was getting upset, as was I.

What every foster kid secretly wants is a family, and to know that we both had that under our noses this whole time was a little hard to hear.

"Well… I just won't be a 'step brother.' I'll be Ruthie's husband. Won't make a difference then," I challenged.

"You look just like your mother. Trust me when I say that she'll know instantly who you are," Able informed me.

I shook my head.

"Well, then I won't go over there at all," I said stiffly.

Able looked at me with all too knowing eyes.

"So you'll withhold your affections from your siblings when it was me and your mother that hurt you?" He asked carefully.

I narrowed my eyes at him.

That was a low blow.

And he knew I'd respond to it.

But not yet.

Now I wanted to know more about why he was here.

"So what were you going to do when you spoke to her? Lead her away from me? You don't even know me," I said, leaning forward.

Ruthie's head met my shoulder, and I wrapped my free arm across her belly to latch onto her hips, hugging her to me as I waited for Able to speak.

Her small hands wrapped around my arm like she would never let me go, and I realized, in that second, that she wouldn't.

It was the first time I let myself realize that, too.

That maybe she felt the same way about me as I felt about her.

That maybe she could deal with my brooding.

She'd run, but I'd always find her.

And I think realizing that I would chase after her had comforted her in some way.

"I would've tried to talk her out of you…after I introduced myself," he said, studying the two of us. "I realize now that there would be no breaking the two of you up, though."

I nodded in confirmation.

He had that right.

Nothing was going to come between us but us.

And that's the way it should be.

Other people didn't need to be in our business, because our business was our own.

"You could've just asked. Maybe sent a letter introducing yourself instead of just throwing it at both of us. You gave Sterling more worry than he needed, at a very bad time that could've gone a lot different had you just introduced yourself more gently. Our last week has been fraught with worry over why you were here and we left things on a bad note," she said to her father. "And that's not something that's going to happen again. If you want us in your life, you need to be the father that you are wanting to become; not one that we'll later realize we don't need."

She totally got me.

She'd realized that I was in a bad place, and she'd let me be. She'd known exactly what was wrong, too. Which helped slam home the earlier point.

She was mine and I'd make her realize it.

Once she realized it, she'd be permanently, and irrevocably mine.

Because I was about to put a freakin' ring on it.

The ringing of Able's phone had our conversation halting, and I knew instantly he was speaking to his wife.

His entire tone had changed.

His body had softened; the wariness went out of his eyes.

Then he said the words.

The ones I that sounded so utterly different when they came from Ruthie's mouth.

"Alright baby. *Ich liebe dich.*"

And it was right then that I decided that the ring would need to come. Soon.

Because I wanted what he had.

I had it…I just needed to make sure it would stay mine. That she'd be with me forever.

CHAPTER 15

If I've offended you, I'll gladly point you in a direction of a dick you can suck.
-Sterling to Cormac

Sterling

Later that night, as I walked into Garrison's guest bedroom, I was thankful.

Thankful that Ruthie had survived.

"Cormac gone?" Ruthie asked from the bed.

"Yeah, he just left," I said, pinching the collar of my t-shirt in order to lift it over my head. "Let him borrow your rental car, though, since it was raining."

I'd gotten Ruthie a rental car on the way home from whatever the hell that was with her father.

We'd driven by the scene of the fire, and looked through what was recovered from the fire that was salvageable.

I hunched my shoulders to help the t-shirt off, and then threw it into the corner of the room.

It hit the wall with a soft plop and fell harmlessly to the floor.

My eyes returned to the bed where Ruthie was now watching me sleepily.

She was propped up on one elbow lying sideways in the bed. She had her hair up in a messy bun on top of her head, and her eyes were heavy with sleep.

She'd been outside with the rest of us until the rest of The Dixie Wardens had filed out of the house.

Once it was just Cormac, Garrison and I left, she gave me a soft kiss on the cheek, waved at the boys, and went to bed without a backward glance, giving us the privacy that she thought we wanted.

Something I would've liked her to do while Silas was here telling me what he'd found out about the fire.

I didn't like that she had to hear about two of her neighbors plotting to set her house on fire.

Didn't like that she'd become so quiet throughout the explanation that I'd been worried that she'd start crying.

I think what helped, though, was the way that my brothers, club and foster alike, had rallied around her in support.

They now knew what she meant to me after my declaration to Silas, just before I went to find Ruthie.

They knew she was my old lady.

Something I had to ask Ruthie soon, because I wanted her to have my name by the time I was deployed for my next mission.

Which could be any day, so I hoped she was amenable.

Plus, having my name would give her some extra protection while I was away.

"I can't believe those two old men plotted in a coffee shop, of all places, about burning my house down. I guess I was lucky that they called the fire department right after they did it," she said as she watched me undress.

No, I guess I couldn't have asked for more... 'ya know, if they were going to burn down a house. It was the least they could do.

I yanked my belt off a little more roughly than I'd intended, and the ends swung and knocked into the wall at my side with the force.

"If you need an outlet for all of that aggression, I've got just the thing for you," she said huskily.

I lifted an eyebrow at her. "You do, do you? And what would that be?"

As she watched, I slowly worked the zipper of my pants down before pushing the jeans from my hips.

My boxerbriefs were the only thing left, and they were doing a terrible job at containing my erection.

The window of fabric that allowed you to whip your dick out, instead of taking your boxers all the way off, was now revealing my cock, and I decided it was time for some new underwear as I walked to the bed.

Her eyes flared as she watched me stalk towards her, and I smiled.

It was purely a predatory smile, one that was meant to throw her off balance.

But my girl wasn't a fluster kind of girl.

She was a take the bull by the horns, kind of girl.

Or, in this instance, the SEAL by the cock.

"You know, you left without saying a word, and it upset me," she said, working her hand into my boxers.

I blinked.

"I told you I had to go, why would it upset you?" I asked, completely dumfounded that she thought I left without 'saying a word.'

"You didn't say goodbye. Didn't say anything the entire night before you left. You didn't make love to me. Didn't say I love you. Didn't even stop me from leaving before you had to leave. Then you didn't call for days," she said, squeezing tightly.

My brain started to short circuit, but I closed my eyes to try to regain some semblance of control.

"I didn't fuck you because, when I got home, you were already asleep. And I thought it'd be kind of rude to wake you up and fuck you when I'd done you all night the night before…which was why I assumed you were sleeping so early. I didn't say goodbye to you because you were all of a sudden gone, and your cell phone was on the table," I said. "And once I got on base, our cell phones go out of range and I can't get anything in or out until I leave, which I told you."

"You did no such thing," she growled.

"What's really your problem?" I asked, pulling gently on her hair to make her look up at me.

"I don't like being ignored. I don't like that you let me leave. I don't like that you didn't say I love you again when that's all I wanted to hear. And I don't like being left out of your thoughts, even though I understood exactly where your mind was at," she whispered.

My eyes softened as I looked down at her, cupping her cheek with one large, scarred hand.

"I do love you. I told you in a note I left for you next to the coffee pot. Didn't you see it?"

She shook her head.

"Well, we can't really look for it now, can we?" I asked, studying her face.

When she shook her head, I let her go and leaned down to place a soft kiss on her lips.

"I've never had anyone to share my problems with before," I told her honestly, staring into those gray eyes that had come to mean so much to me. "But I'll try to let you in. I won't shut you out anymore...okay?"

Then she cupped my balls, and I lost all desire to think.

"What are you doing?" I asked, nearly choking as she bent down and sucked the very tip of my cock into her wet mouth.

And my desire to let her have control of me flew out the window along with all propriety on how a woman should be treated.

"Turn onto your back and let your head dangle over the edge," I ordered gruffly, looking down at the top of her head as she bobbed on my cock.

She looked up, smiled with her eyes, and slowly let my cock fall from her suctioning mouth with a soft pop before she shucked her clothes.

Then she laid on the bed and scooted until her head fell off the side of the bed, putting that lovely, succulent mouth in the perfect position to take my cock deep into the back of her throat.

"Open," I said, running the tip of my cock along the closed seam of her mouth.

She did, but only enough to allow her insanely talented tongue out.

I ran the length of my cock up and down her tongue, smiling when I saw the mirth in her eyes.

"So you want to play, do you?" I asked.

She winked at me, then lifted her hands to come to a rest at the backs of my thighs.

When they slowly moved up and started to curve inside, I bent down, letting my cock rest against her face, and bit her lightly on the stomach.

She yelped.

"Too rough?" I asked. "I thought you wanted to play."

I felt her head move in between my thighs, then her mouth was on my balls, tugging lightly on the sensitive skin with her sharp little teeth.

I gasped.

"Playful enough for you?" She teased, then licked the seam of my balls as far back as she could reach.

"I think the blood's draining to your head at an alarming rate if you think biting a man on the balls is playful," I said breathlessly.

I wasn't feeling playful anymore. I was feeling need. Desperation. Want. Desire.

Playful wasn't one of them.

All with one little move on her part, and all of my nice bones in my body had been replaced by desperate ones.

Something I showed her when I dove face first into her pussy and started to eat her with a voraciousness that surprised her.

"Sterling," she gasped, widening her legs for my face.

When her legs spread, the lips of her sex spread as well, giving me unhindered access to everything I wanted right at that moment.

I plunged my tongue deep inside her waiting pussy, unsurprised that she was already wet for me.

I'd never found her not wet for me…not needy and wanting.

"You like when I suck your little clit?" I rasped against her pussy.

"Yes," she said, running the tip of her tongue up the length of my cock. "I love it when you put your hands on me. Your mouth and tongue on me."

"You do?" I asked, snaking my hand underneath her ass and curving it around until my fingers could plunge into her pussy without disrupting the work I was doing on her clit.

She gasped when I sank two fingers inside of her, and I groaned when my cock was finally granted access to what it wanted most.

Her heat.

It wasn't picky.

Anything that was hot and wet was good enough.

Her mouth. Her pussy. Soon to be her ass.

Every hole in her body was mine to do with as I pleased, and she'd find that out.

Soon.

Because I was feeling particularly frantic today, and claiming all that was Ruthie was going to make the unbearable feeling of almost losing her last night better.

I started to pump my cock in and out of her mouth as I let my fingers swirl in her wetness that was drenching my hand.

"Ruthie," I said, pulling my cock back out of her mouth. "Has anybody ever had all of your holes?"

She clenched down on my fingers as I started to pull them free of her pussy, and I smiled against her thigh.

"I take that as you like the idea of it…but you didn't answer my question," I rumbled, placing a wet kiss on her thigh.

"N-no," she answered, her hot breath blowing on my cock like a cool caress.

I moved my fingers down to rest against her back entrance, pressing in slightly with one finger, gauging her reaction.

She moaned loudly before sucking my cock back into her mouth.

Her hands traveled up the outsides of my thighs moving up and down with the movement of her mouth on my cock.

I licked her clit, then sucked the tiny bundle of nerves into my mouth as I sank one finger inside of her ass.

Her entrance resisted for a long moment, but with each suck of her clit, she relaxed more and more until I was finally able to get inside of her.

"God," she moaned around my dick.

Or, at least, that's what I assumed she said.

I really couldn't be sure when her mouth was that full.

I moved my finger past the first ring of muscle, my own gut clenching in need as I felt the tightness just from one of my fingers.

I couldn't wait to see what it felt like when I had my cock buried deep, pounding away inside of her forbidden entrance.

She backed off my cock, and I used the change to pull back until I could move around the bed and climb on between her legs on the opposite side, all the while keeping my finger buried deep.

Awkward, but it worked.

"Scoot back," I rasped, grabbing a hold of her thigh with my free hand and helping her until her head rested on the bed once again.

She looked down between her legs, watching as I moved my middle finger in and out of her back passage.

"You want more?" I asked, careful not to give her too much to handle at once.

She nodded.

"Yeah," she croaked, both of her hands going to her tits to play with her nipples.

I bit my lip and gathered some more of her wetness with another finger before easing that one inside of her, too.

Her eyes closed, and she bit her lip to keep the moan from rattling the blinds in the room with her intensity.

"God," she breathed once I started to move. "I never thought this would be this good."

So she'd never had that asshole husband of hers do this for her.

Interesting.

"Does it feel good, baby?" I asked, leaning forward to pull one of her nipples into my mouth.

She fed it to me, moving her hand to my face once I got a good latch and started to suck.

Her fingers ran along my beard, and she started to moan intently as I moved my fingers in and out of her.

When I felt her muscles starting to tense in the beginnings of an orgasm, I pulled out of her completely and shoved my fat cock inside her willing pussy.

Coating my cock in her juices as her orgasm overtook her.

I pounded deep inside of her, working her over and over again until she was about ready to fall over the cliff a second time.

And when she finally did, I pulled out of her abruptly, lined my cock up against her ass, and slowly eased inside.

She came.

The pain and pleasure of my entrance pushed her over the edge once again, and her pulsing channel about made my eyes cross with the tightness.

Once her orgasm receded, then her pain synapses started to kick back online.

My thumb flicked her clit as the pain from my entrance started to overtake her.

I could tell she was at war with herself.

Taking a cock in the ass wasn't something that all women liked, nor could they do.

But based on how she'd responded to my fingers, I knew it'd be good for her once she got used to my cock inside the tight sheath of her ass.

"Fuck," Ruthie said. "It burns."

I moved my thumb faster as I held extremely still in her ass, letting her adjust even though every instinct inside of me was urging me to fuck her hard and fast.

"Okay," she whispered.

I opened my eyes that I hadn't realized I closed, and looked down into hers.

"Okay?" I asked.

She nodded, biting her lip once more.

"I'm okay, move," she whispered. "*Slowly*."

I nodded, bending down onto one stiffened arm and slowly started to move, pulling and pushing back and forth, giving her a little taste of how good it could be.

She moaned, lifting her hips to meet my thrusts, and I smiled.

"Like it?" I asked.

She nodded, moving her hand down to her pussy and slowly sinking two fingers inside.

"Yeah, I like it," she whispered.

I groaned at the erotic feeling of her fingers massaging not only herself, but me at the same time.

And when she started to come once again, I finally let go, pounding my cock inside of her ass just like I'd wanted to.

Giving her my entire length.

Her breasts bounced with my thrusts, and her eyes closed.

I grunted as my release shot out of my cock, filling up her ass with all that was me.

Satisfaction coursed through my veins at having claimed her fully, and my cock felt drained by the time the last spurt of come left my cock.

"God," she breathed once I stopped. "I never knew."

I leaned down and kissed her, pressing my length inside of her fully.

She moaned into my mouth.

"You undo me," I told her.

She hugged my neck tightly.

"Ditto."

I snorted and pulled back, letting my cock pop free of her and started to walk backwards on my knees out of the bed.

I smiled when I saw how sated she looked, and it sent emotions pouring through me that I never realized I had.

Happiness. Hope. Contentedness. Love. Want.

When my eyes finally met hers once they traveled up her body, she said, "*Ich liebe dich.*"

"Ditto," I said, pulling her foot until she was resting on the edge of the bed.

Once she was close enough, I gathered her into my arms and walked with her into the bathroom.

I set her on the counter while I got the shower started, then picked her up once more to carry her into the shower with me.

She washed me gently. *Lovingly.*

And never did it occur to me that all of this would disappear in the next hour.

That my life would be turned upside down once again.

That I'd be left with a bloody, gaping hole in my heart that would change my life completely.

CHAPTER 16

You make me happy when skies are gray. And when they're not gray. Even when they're green...which means a tornado's coming. Which typically isn't something to be happy about.
-Ruthie to Sterling

Ruthie

"The next of kin is listed as this address. Are you Cormac Austin's brothers?" The state trooper had asked.

Garrison and Sterling nodded.

"I'm Garrison, and this is Sterling," Garrison said, introducing himself.

They'd both answered the door together.

I'd heard it, as had Sterling, and I shouldn't have been surprised that Sterling went out of the room.

But as I listened to the seriousness of the trooper's voice, I was glad he did.

"Yes, we're his brothers" Sterling answered.

"Parents?" The trooper asked.

Garrison shook his head. "No we're all each other has."

The trooper nodded, then looked down at his hands before he looked back up at the two men in front of him.

I could see him from where I was standing behind the two of them.

The couch was in front of me, and the moment the words left his mouth,

I clutched onto the sofa with both hands.

"Cormac Austin died at the Louisiana/Texas border. Since his next of kin were on my side, I'm the one to deliver the news. At one eighteen this morning, he was hit head on by a semi-truck when Cormac attempted to avoid a stalled car in the roadway. He was killed on impact," the trooper said.

My knees gave out at the pure devastation that was roaring through my body.

Oh, my God.

"No," somebody moaned.

It could've been me.

Garrison.

Sterling.

I didn't know.

What I did know was that Sterling was about to fucking lose it.

I knew that with one look at his taut body.

The way he held himself.

The way his body rocked back and forth.

I turned to the bedroom, going straight to where I'd seen Sterling plug his phone into the wall earlier when we'd come into the room.

Then immediately pulled up the first person on his call list.

Loki.

I tapped his name and hit send, closing my eyes as I listened to Garrison's shocked voice come to me from the living room.

Sterling's voice wasn't heard, but I knew…I knew he needed his family right now.

And they would come.

"Hello?" A grumpy voice answered.

"Loki," I gasped in a tear filled voice. "I need you to come back over. I need you and anyone else you can get. Sterling's about to lose it. Cormac's dead."

"Be there in five."

Then he hung up.

I dropped the phone and ran back into the living room to see the door closing behind the trooper.

Garrison looked white as a ghost.

Sterling didn't look anything.

He was just blank.

Which didn't last for long when he stalked past me and into the room, returning moments later with his cut on over his bare skin, and the key to his motorcycle in his hand.

"Where are you going?" I asked.

"Out."

I stopped him by putting my back to the door, blocking it.

Although I knew it wouldn't work very well, and that he could get past me easily, he stopped.

Mostly for my benefit, I was sure, but I couldn't let him leave.

Not like this.

Not in this state of mind.

"Where are you going?" I asked again.

"To a bar. I need to get drunk," he said stiffly.

I raised a brow at him. "Do you think that'll help right now? Look at Garrison. Do you think he needs you to go drinking when he needs you?"

Sterling stared blankly at me.

Garrison snorted. "I can take care of myself; actually, a drink sounds pretty fucking amazing right now."

With that he disappeared into his room that was off the living room, and returned moments later with a t-shirt on and his feet rammed into boots sloppily.

Sterling never moved, staring at me like he didn't even know me.

I just knew this was a horrible idea.

A really bad, no good one.

These two didn't need to go get drunk.

They could get drunk here…but not out where they could potentially ruin their lives…ruin someone else's lives.

Then Sterling started towards me, and I knew instantly he wasn't going to stop.

I moved out of the way, knowing if I stayed there he'd just move me…or plow right through me.

But then only seconds after the door was yanked open by Sterling, I heard the blissful sound of pipes.

Multiple ones.

Coming up to Garrison's house fast.

I closed my eyes in relief as first Loki, then Trance, followed shortly by

Sebastian pulled up into the front of Garrison's house.

"Fuck," Sterling hissed. "Motherfuck!"

I visibly cringed when Sterling turned his now very pissed off eyes to me.

My body slid behind Garrison's porch post, and I hid my face so Sterling could no longer see me directly.

The light from the porch wasn't on, and the streetlight only did so much.

Which meant he couldn't see my tear filled eyes at what that look had done to me.

God.

This was horrible.

More bikes pulled up, and I finally felt it was okay to go into the house, knowing that they wouldn't let him do anything stupid.

My feet took me into the kitchen where I grabbed a bottle of water from the fridge and took it into the bedroom that Garrison had given the two of us to sleep in.

I fell face first into the comforter, then cried my little heart out until I felt the bed dip.

I turned my tear filled eyes to see Sawyer standing there, with Lily behind her.

"Hey," I croaked.

***

Two hours later, the tequila that Sawyer had been able to confiscate from the boys outside started talking.

"It's my fault. Had the fire not happened...they wouldn't have even been here," I whispered to Sawyer and Lily.

Lily hugged me tightly.

"It's not your fault you have psycho neighbors," she whispered.

Tears coursed down my face, and I pulled away from her.

"It is. If I'd never had come…" I shook my head.

"If you'd never have come, I wouldn't be here right now."

My eyes closed.

Sterling's voice sounded low and devastated.

Pain practically dripped from each of his words, but when I turned to look at him, he looked unaffected.

"What?" I asked. "Why would you say that?"

"Because you're what kept me alive during that mission. You're what had me going…I pulled every one of my team out of a hostile situation. Everyone but me was down…and you were the only one that kept me going. Your eyes. Your smile. Your voice. You. Had it not been for you, I, and all of them, would've been dead," he explained softly.

The tears on my cheeks started to cool, and I looked at him wide eyed.

"You never said," I whispered.

He shrugged as if it made no difference. "I'm not allowed to tell you. I'm not even allowed to tell you that I had a debriefing three days ago."

And he was telling me now, because he didn't want me to blame myself.

But I still did.

But it was obvious that I needed to be more careful what I said in front of him.

"Thank you," I said. "Can I get you anything?"

"A new heart?" He asked, laughing humorlessly. "Mine seems to be broken at the moment."

I stood up, feeling Sawyer and Lily slip their hands off my shoulders as I went.

Then walked straight to my man and wrapped him in a hug so tight that it would've broken any other person.

Not my Sterling, though.

He was solid.

Formidable.

Unbreakable.

"You okay?" I asked softly.

I could smell the whiskey on his breath.

And I was sure he could smell the tequila on mine.

"No…" he whispered into my hair as he wrapped his arms around me. "I'm not even a little bit okay."

"I'm so sorry," I breathed, hugging him even tighter.

He took the hug, and gave as good as he got.

"I'm ready to pass out and forget," he said.

I looked up into his eyes.

"Okay. We'll think about the rest tomorrow."

Because there were plans to be made.

I'd already heard about him and Garrison having to go up to the morgue tomorrow and identify Cormac's body.

Funeral arrangements.

I felt Lily's lips on my cheek, followed shortly by Sawyer's hug that captured both me and Sterling.

"Your girls are weird," he rumbled once they left.

"They love you," I told him.

He took a deep breath.

"Yeah."

"Let's go to bed," I whispered.

Maybe tomorrow would look better, because surely one couple couldn't suffer anymore…right?

Wrong.

CHAPTER 17

When a woman starts a sentence off with, "I just find it funny..."
That means you should run. Fast. Because nothing is remotely
funny to her. In fact, it's the exact fucking opposite.
-Words of wisdom

Ruthie

Two days later

I'd never been in a biker procession before.

Never seen the sheer perfectness of it.

Never would I have thought that grief would just slip away.

Not permanently...*but for now.*

Which was good enough.

I'd take just about anything right now to make this heartache stop
hurting...especially for Sterling.

His hand on my thigh tightened, and I looked up to see the hearse that
was carrying Cormac's body turn the turn signal on, then take a right into
the cemetery where he would be buried.

We'd been going about thirty miles an hour for about an hour now, and I
couldn't say whether I was thankful or not that we were finally here.

The funeral had already taken place, and now we were following the
hearse to the cemetery that would forever be the home of Cormac's
body.

Garrison and Sterling had shelled out quite a bit to get him into this cemetery, supposedly it'd been a very popular one and people had to be put on a waiting list to get in there.

It wasn't like it was a country club or anything, but if that was where they wanted, that was where they'd get.

We were the first bike of about seventy five who pulled up into the parking spots directly in front of the gate.

A huge tent like structure had already been erected about a half a football field away from the front entrance, and I only assumed that was where we were headed.

"You ready?" Sterling asked me.

I nodded. "Yeah, ready when you are."

He nodded and held out his hand for me to dismount, following suit moments later once I was standing next to him wearing my new dress pants and dark purple shirt I'd gotten at Target the day before.

Sterling was in his dress whites, a dilemma since he wasn't sure whether he should wear his dress whites, or his dress blues.

Eventually, he'd called and asked, where we'd learned that he could wear either one.

And although I knew why he didn't want to wear white for the overall feeling of the funeral, I still think he'd made a good decision with the whites since those had been the ones he'd been leaning towards.

Not to mention it was extremely hot and either one would've been uncomfortable.

Sweat was pouring down his face, and I could tell he was extremely uncomfortable.

"Come on," Sterling said. "I want to get into position before they start moving him."

I understood why he wanted to minutes later when he stood in a perfect salute, hand at a perfect ninety degrees.

Six of ULM's baseball team members moved to the back of the hearse, and as one they hauled the casket from the back.

He stayed that way as the coffin was moved from the back of the hearse, down the pathway leading to the grave, and stopped once they'd reached the graveside stand that would hold the coffin for the remainder of the service.

My throat felt like there was a golf ball lodged deep in it, and I couldn't help but study Sterling's face.

He looked unaffected by it all, but I knew for a fact that he *was* affected.

Deeply.

This was the face that he showed the world when he didn't want anyone to see what he was feeling.

The face that he'd perfected when he was a young boy trying to stay alive.

When the rest of the gathering finally gathered close, Sterling latched onto my hand, almost making me wince with his intensity.

"As we all gather here today, I'd like to go ahead and say thank you one more time for attending. This gathering by the graveside is a celebration. Of what a beautiful life our Cormac had."

Sterling's hand tensed, and I knew instantly what he was thinking.

Cormac hadn't had a nice life, just like Garrison and Sterling hadn't.

He'd had a shit life, and it'd ended too soon.

"His best friends have requested that they speak. Now, if you'll turn your attention to this young man over here, we'll get started," the officiator said.

Sterling gave my hand a slight squeeze and let me go, moving up to the front for all to see him.

Sawyer took up one side of me, while Garrison took up the other, and together we watched as Sterling poured his heart out.

"Cormac made me promise that I would chop his head off and burn his body once he died so he couldn't be brought back as a zombie," Sterling said, looking down at his hands. "I thought I'd never have to tell him that I'd never do that for him, because zombies weren't real."

I closed my eyes as a tear spilled over my cheek.

The first of many.

"We didn't do that, in case you're wondering," Sterling said, looking up at the crowd.

A small ripple of laughter coursed over the gathering.

I hated funerals.

They were so sad.

Everything about them made me sick to my stomach.

The crying.

The flowers.

The sea of black on all of the mourners.

Then there was the baseball team for ULM.

Every one of them was dressed in their baseball uniforms, and they held their hats in their laps as they looked down at their feet.

"I did wear this stupid uniform, even though it's nearly a hundred and ten degrees out. He made me promise that I would wear a bright color to his funeral," he said, laughing slightly. "Again, I never thought I'd have to worry about it. I always thought I'd be the first one to die."

Garrison, at my side, made a choking sound, and I placed my hand on his, which he grabbed on to and held onto for dear life.

His body shook, and I wanted to wrap my hands around the big, scary man.

"Cormac, Garrison, and I were like The Three Musketeers.

"I'd had them, and only them, to depend on for a good long while until I met the rest of my family," he said, leaning his head in the direction of all the bikers that were at my back.

Men who'd taken Sterling in and helped mold the man he was today.

"I thought we'd grow old together. Raise our kids together. Sit out on the back deck and drink beer. I thought we'd finally won when I heard he was trying out for a major league team…and I was going to ask the woman I love to marry me. I thought we'd won."

My heart broke.

And as listened to the rest of Sterling's eulogy, I knew that today would forever mark him.

Forever be a day in his mind that meant he'd failed.

But he wasn't a failure, not even a little bit.

***

"Hello?" Sterling answered his phone.

Then his jaw clenched.

"Yeah, I can be there by nightfall," Sterling answered.

I looked over at him quickly, and saw his eyes focused on me.

My stomach sank.

He was being called in for another mission.

Shit.

Then, right in the middle of everyone at the dinner after Cormac's funeral, Sterling dropped down to one knee.

"I didn't want to ask you this here…I thought I had more time," he whispered to me. "But I need to ask you before I go…just in case."

Just in case he dies, I thought bitterly.

"Will you marry me?" He asked softly.

My eyes watered, and I closed my eyes as tears started to pour down my cheeks in great torrents.

"Yeah, I'll marry you," I said, opening my eyes to take him in.

He slipped the beautiful ring on my finger, then moved until he was standing directly in front of me.

"We'll get married when I get home," he ordered.

I nodded. "Okay."

"You'll listen to Silas…and the rest of them, okay?" He asked.

I nodded.

I knew he'd worry if I didn't say yes, so I agreed, even though it bristled.

"You'll make sure you answer my calls, no matter where you're at," he continued.

I snorted. "Absolutely I will. Like you'd get me not to."

He moved forward and pressed his lips softly against mine.

"I love you," he whispered.

I gave him the words.

Words that had come to mean a whole lot more to me lately.

"I love you, too."

He turned without another word and walked out the door, stopping in front of Silas and Garrison.

"You'll protect her."

It wasn't a question, but another demand.

Both men nodded. "You know we will."

His head hung for five long seconds, then he straightened his back and walked out without another backward glance.

Into the dangerous world of a Navy SEAL.

CHAPTER 18

Some heroes wear a cape. Mine wear's camo.
-Ruthie to a stranger

Ruthie

Day 4

I got the confirmation that he was where he was supposed to be.

That was good, wasn't it?

You know what wasn't good?

Being followed to my job.

And home.

And to the freakin' bathroom.

That wasn't good.

***

Day 12

Kraken (2:22): I'm okay.

Ruthie (2:22): Why does your name say Kraken?

Kraken (2:22): Because I'm the sea monster...or so I've been told.

Ruthie (2:23): The one that ruins everyone's day?

Kraken (2:23): Funny funny.

Ruthie (2:24): How come I don't know where you are?

Kraken (2:25): You'll never know where I am.

Ruthie (2:26): Well that just sucks.

Kraken (2:27): You knew what you signed up for. You're mine for eternity.

Ruthie (2:27): I wasn't thinking clearly.

Kraken (2:28): Your loss and my gain. No take backs.

Ruthie (2:30): That's not funny. I miss you.

Ruthie (2:35): Kraken, are you done with me?

Ruthie (3:22): I love you Sterling, come home to me in one piece or else.

***

Day 32

Kraken (5:15): Or else what?

Ruthie (5:22): Really? You're going to finish a conversation from twenty days ago?

Kraken (5:23): Shit happens.

Ruthie (5:25): You catch your bad guy yet?

Kraken (5:26): Working on it.

Ruthie (5:27): That's helpful.

Kraken (5:28): I try.

Kraken (5:29): Going again. Love you too.

***

Day 44

"Hello?" I answered tiredly.

I'd worked a double shift today at Dane's, then a single shift at Halligans

232

and Handcuffs.

I'd literally worked myself into the ground in hopes that I wouldn't have to be at home long before I fell asleep once again.

It was easier that way.

And I'd been asleep for nearly two hours when my phone rang.

It was now eleven fifty three at night, and if it wasn't someone important on the phone, I'd start losing my shit.

"This Ruthie?" A gruff man's voice asked.

He sounded like he was a chain smoker his voice was so rough.

"Yeah, this is Ruthie," I answered.

"This is Parker, I'm here with Sterling," he said.

I blinked. "Then why isn't Sterling calling me?"

"Because he's running a fever like a little fuckin' girl, and he won't take the fuckin' meds I'm trying to give him because he's hallucinating. So I'm calling you to talk to him in hopes that he'll unclench his fuckin' teeth and take his fuckin' meds," Parker explained tightly.

I blinked. "Why is he running a fever?"

The Parker guy sighed.

"I'm not at liberty to tell you," he answered stiffly.

"Was he shot? Is he hurt? Tell me!" I demanded.

"My God, you're as bad as him, blowing stuff way out of proportion," Parker grumbled.

"Ruthie?" A seriously sluggish sounding Sterling called.

"Sterling? Hey baby, are you okay?" I asked.

"'m fine. Whatchoo doin' right now?" He asked.

I laughed softly under my breath.

"I was sleeping." I told him.

"Good. At least one of us should be sleepin.' 'm so freakin' tired I could sleep for a month," he whispered. "'s it okay?"

"Is what okay, honey?" I asked.

"To take the medicine," he groaned.

"Yeah, baby. It's okay," I answered.

"Good," he said. "'Cause I didn't want to be killed by taking some terrorists medicine."

With that he said, "'Luh you." And hung up.

I started to freak the fuck out, because the moment I said that, I started to think of 'what if.'

What if that guy wasn't on Sterling's team?

What if that was a terrorist?

What if he wasn't really sick?

I tried to call the number back, but it immediately went to voicemail.

The next number I called was immediately sent to voicemail.

"Fuck you, too, Silas," I growled, flicking to the next name on the list.

Loki.

"Hello?" Loki asked, sounding tired.

"Do you know a guy named Parker?"

"Yeah, fucker slit my throat."

I gasped, my stomach dropping in dismay.

"Oh, no," I moaned. "Oh, God. I told Sterling to take the medicine that Parker was offering him."

I hadn't realized I was hyperventilating until Loki started yelling at me.

"Ruthie!" Loki bellowed.

I put the phone back to my ear.

"Yeah?" I whispered forlornly.

"He's on Sterling's team."

I closed my eyes and let my head drop to my hands.

"Thank God."

"What was the call about?" Loki asked once I'd calmed down somewhat.

"He was running a fever and the man, Parker, wanted to give him meds but he wouldn't take it without talking to me," I answered.

"Got it. Don't freak out. He's fine."

It wasn't until much later that I realized I'd never gotten around to asking Loki what he meant by Parker slitting his throat.

Was that how he'd gotten that scar?

Needless to say, I didn't sleep so well that night, worrying about Sterling and whether or not I'd have to kick this Parker guy's ass for slitting Loki's throat.

***

Day 54

Kraken (10:22): I'm fine.

Ruthie (10:24): You better be.

Kraken (10:25): I am, promise.

Ruthie (10:26): What happened?

Kraken (10:27): Don't drink Iraq's water.

Ruthie (10:28): That's not funny.

Kraken (10:28): Trust me, I'm not being funny.

Ruthie (10:30): When are you coming home?

Ruthie (10:42): Sterling?

Ruthie (12:22): Shit hell piss.

***

Day 63

It'd been sixty-three days since I'd seen Sterling.

And in that sixty-three days, a lot had happened.

I'd rented the house across the street from Garrison and moved what minimal things I had into it.

I'd started school.

Sawyer had had her baby.

I'd worked.

Mostly, though, I'd listened.

Which was a good thing, because I'd learned all kinds of things.

Such as the fact that Sterling was on another dangerous mission that involved the same senator's wife that he'd been on months before.

I'd also learned that Cormac's death wasn't an accident.

That somebody had cut the brake lines on my car expertly, which had contributed to why he hadn't been able to stop.

Which I'd found out only moments before during a party celebrating the birth of Silas and Sawyer's child.

Apparently bikers tended to have chatty, loose lips when they were three sheets to the wind.

Which had a lot to do with why I had heard in the first place.

Silas and the rest of The Dixie Wardens were pretty tight lipped about things when they didn't want their women to know.

And since Sterling wasn't here to tell me, the bunch of badass bikers, and one really annoying baseball coach, had taken it upon themselves to hide it from me as they discussed whether it was a good idea to tell Sterling.

I'd stood listening outside the door that Baylee, Sebastian's wife, had told me was 'church.'

Somewhere where the members went to discuss important matters that involved other people's lives except their own.

"Debated on whether to tell him anything…" Silas muttered darkly.

My mouth dropped open as I listened to Silas tell the group about how the brake lines on Cormac's car were purposefully cut.

"You can't tell him. If he finds out, he'll be focusing on what's going on at home instead of what's going on there," I declared, bursting through the door.

"He deserves to know," Garrison defended, surprising me.

"And do you remember the last freakin' mission he went on? Do you really want to add to the burden right now by telling him that Cormac's death wasn't an accident, but murder?" I hissed.

"I think that you should let him decide that," Sterling said angrily from behind me.

I winced.

Maybe I should've scanned the room before I went bursting into rooms.

Then again…one would think that the man that loved her would've told her he was home instead of hiding out in a room!

"What are you doing here?" I yelled somewhat irately.

His brows lifted at my tone.

"Where else would I be?" He asked.

I stomped my foot. "In Iraq?" I asked snottily.

"I got home," he explained.

"And what…" I asked. "You weren't planning on telling me?"

"I would've told you…had you arrived on time," he growled.

I narrowed my eyes at him.

"I had to work! What'd you want me to do? Leave early just because there was a party going on…one in which I didn't know you were going to be at?" I asked. "Why would I want to be around here when every single one of them," I said, pointing my fingers at the men on either side of him. "Remind me of you. Do you know how torturous that is?"

The nerve!

Then he smiled!

Smiled!

"I missed you too, Ruthie," he said. "Now come here and give me a freakin' hug."

I ran and threw myself into his arms.

My body hit his so hard that he bumped backwards against the wall, but he held me tightly throughout.

"I hate that you're gone so much," I whispered to him.

He kissed my forehead.

"It's my job, baby," he whispered.

"I know," I told him. "It still sucks, though. Don't do anything stupid, either," I continued.

He leaned back from me.

"Whatever I do won't be stupid, honey. What I do will be justice. For Cormac," he insisted.

"Yeah, but he wouldn't want you to be going to jail, a place I know you won't like. Nor would he want you to be dishonorably discharged from the SEALS, when Lord knows he was so proud of you for accomplishing that honor," I informed him.

He leaned forward and kissed my forehead.

"We'll see," he said. "Looks like they've got the guy anyway."

I scowled. "Who was it?"

He looked at me warily before turning me to look at a picture I'd not noticed sitting on the table.

And my whole world dropped, and I fainted.

Fucking fainted.

CHAPTER 19

If you don't want to be with me because I'm loud and speak my mind, fine. Go be with that boring bitch who'll probably only give you missionary and never suck you off. You deserve the bitch and her Hamburger Helper.
-Ruthie's secret thoughts

Ruthie

My eyes were wide as they stared at the man that had been partially responsible for me marrying Bender.

"What...why...how?" I asked Bender's father, aghast that he was even standing in front of me.

Well...sitting. He was currently being held in a sort of cell type thing that was at the Dixie Warden clubhouse.

His hands were in cuffs on the table in front of him, and he was really not happy to see me.

I hadn't seen him in years upon years, and he was all of a sudden here? Why?

John, Bender's father, glared at me.

"Why should you be happy when my boy is dead and in the cold ground? I never should've listened to Reena," he growled.

"What are you talking about?" I asked, startled.

"But no, I did, because I loved her. Then look where it got us. Bender dead. Our grandkid dead. All because you couldn't keep your fucking legs closed," he hissed.

My spine straightened. "What are you talking about?"

"I couldn't believe it when I got the letter saying you were let out," he hissed. "You were supposed to be in there for another year before I had to worry about you getting out. Then there was the letter, and Reena started to freak out about it all. She wouldn't leave well enough alone. Things would have worked out. I would have had you taken care of but she just had to get me involved right now. So I had to come take care of it...of you...before you could make this world even worse than it already is. But those stupid neighbors of yours...fucked everything up. Bunch of imbeciles. So here I am, sitting in a jail cell when I should've been at home with my wife."

I looked over to the man that was to become my husband and raised a questioning brow at him.

He gestured to the other room, and I turned on my heel and left, leaving John where he sat in his chair, fuming at being manhandled by a bunch of 'biker scum.'

"How'd he get here?" I asked in confusion. "And why's he here instead of at the police station?"

Sterling turned and gestured to the far side of the room, and my eyebrows probably lined up with my hairline as I saw who was leaning against the wall.

"What are you doing here?" I asked Able.

"That was an apology," Able said sincerely to Sterling.

Sterling's face was once again blank.

"What do you mean, it was an apology?" I asked in confusion.

"Came home, saw my wife looking at a baby picture of Sterling again, and realized that I'd fucked up. Knew that I should've fixed it years ago, but it was seeing you with my girl that made me realize that I would've given anything for time with her, and I'd purposefully kept you from her all these years," he said sincerely.

My eyes watered.

So much time was lost, for both Sterling and me, with our respective parent.

How would our life be had we known each other from the moment we were younger?

Definitely not about to be married, that's what.

"So you what…just found the guy that The Dixie Wardens MC couldn't find? How is that possible? I thought you were an oil man. What kind of skills does an oil man have that can find a man who even trained professionals can't find?" I asked.

Able's face continued to stay blank, but his eyes were saying something completely different.

"That's because he's not just an oil tycoon. He's a fucking hit man," Silas said from behind us.

I turned in surprise.

"What?" I gasped.

Silas nodded. "Took me a while. Had my hands full or we would've found out about John Wait before…but my resources were split trying to find out about you, too. So it took longer than I would've liked. Ended up that we found him at the same time, but I wanted to see Able's skills, just what he was capable of, so we let him bring John in."

"You're a freakin' hit man?" I asked, spinning around to stare at my 'father.'

He winced. "Was, yes."

"What…how…why?" I asked. "And why come back? What are you hoping to accomplish?"

"I was hoping to accomplish a relationship with my daughter that I've done nothing but think about for the last fifteen years. I was hoping that, one day, I'd be able to see her smile again like I had when she was just a girl. And I'm not a 'hit man' per se. I'm a contract agent for the United States Government. Bit of a difference," he said defensively.

I shook my head, the beginnings of a headache forming at the base of my neck.

"This is all so fucked up. So completely fucked up," I said, shaking my head, rubbing my neck with my hand as I closed my eyes.

Firm, warm hands captured my head, and I was pulled firmly into Sterling's arms.

"You wanna go home?" He asked softly.

"Yeah," I answered. "I do."

"Then let's do it."

So we left everyone behind.

Things were far from over with both John and Able.

But I really, *really* just wanted to lay in Sterling's arms right then, and forget the world around us.

Tomorrow we'd deal with the rest.

Tomorrow we'd face what I didn't want to face today.

***

"Does it make us dirty?" I asked softly as Sterling got into the bed next to me.

"Does what make us dirty?" He asked, groaning when his back finally found purchase on the bed.

It was a nice bed.

I'd gotten a little help from Sterling's hefty bank account to furnish the house.

I'd gotten a new fridge, washer and dryer, dishwasher and bed.

The rest was thrift store finest, but it would do for now.

I knew he'd want a nice bed, and I wanted to make sure that he had it.

I wanted him to have everything that he ever wanted.

"That we're step brother and step sister," I whispered, rolling over until I could look into his tired face.

He was tanner than when he'd left.

And he had a new scar on his hand that I'd never seen before…one that I assumed was the reason for his fever.

I didn't bother to ask how he'd gotten such an ugly scar.

The less I knew, the better.

His eyes opened when I said 'step sister.'

"It's not dirty since we didn't even know our parents were married. It'd only be dirty if we'd known each other since we were five and used to take baths together," he answered sincerely.

I grinned.

"I don't know," I said, letting my hands roam up his sides as I sat up and straddled his hips.

His cock instantly started to harden as he took me in, looking me up and down.

I was wearing one of his t-shirts, a black one with the Punisher Skull on it.

My ass was bare, seeing as he seemed to make my panties disintegrate, and since I was somewhat fond of my panties, I decided to circumvent the inevitable and just gone without.

My breasts were free under my shirt, not just because Sterling was just as rough with my bras as he was with my panties, but because bras were just plain uncomfortable all the way around.

His hands went up to my hips, holding me tightly as he ground his erection up into me.

"I missed you," I said softly, looking down into his eyes.

He'd shaved his beard to more manageable levels than what he'd come home with, and I found that I missed the scruffiness.

Although I liked him clean cut, too, I also liked him a little bit wild.

"I missed you too. Scared shitless about what I'd come home to, but I knew that my brothers would take care of you," he murmured, running his hand up over the flat expanse of my belly, to come to a rest in between my breasts.

"What did Silas have to say?" I asked.

Silas had followed us home, and had spoken to Sterling while I'd taken a quick shower and started dinner.

I'd nearly finished with it by the time he'd shown, freshly showered and ready to eat.

"Just explaining a little more on John," he answered evasively.

I narrowed my eyes at him.

"What about him?" I asked.

He shrugged.

"Well," he hesitated.

I glared. "Tell me."

"Not really much to tell. He wanted you back in prison, and he was hoping that by making you 'break the law' he'd get you back there. Except he didn't really count on us. He thought that by you getting in trouble with the law, it'd break your parole agreement," he said finally. "The more stuff you got away with, the uglier he got until he was more desperate than not. Cutting your brakes," his voice broke. "That was a spur of the moment thing. After all his other attempts at getting people to manipulate you, he took it into his own hands and finally took care of matters himself."

I closed my eyes, and suddenly I wasn't feeling anything but sorrow.

It really was my fault.

"I'm so sorry," I whispered as tears started to brim at the lids of my eyes. "I never would've thought he'd go that far. He was always so laid back. He was there in the courtroom when I was being sentenced. He didn't even look upset."

I felt lower than low.

But Sterling's hands on my face jolted me out of my misery as he took my face in his hands and shook me slightly.

"Stop it," he demanded. "Stop it now."

I blinked.

"What?" I asked, tears starting to slip over.

"You need to get your mind off of whatever happened. I hate to say it…" he started. "But I'm glad it wasn't you. It makes me a terrible person…but I'm fucking glad it wasn't you."

I face planted into his chest, and I cried.

For the loss we'd suffered.

The injustice of it all.

For everything.

My life had been absolute shit.

Wasn't it fucking time that something went right?

Didn't I deserve it?

Didn't we deserve it?

"I'm so fucking over this life, Sterling," I said into his chest.

"You're not done with it until I say you're done with it," he growled, rolling over with me until I was underneath him.

My hips were cradling his thighs, and he was looking down at me with such ferocity that I couldn't breathe.

"Okay," I said breathlessly.

"You're mine and I'm yours. We'll make our lives good together. We'll have babies. We'll buy a house. We'll grow old together until we can't see the other's faults. We'll be together forever. And then, when we're done on this earth, we'll go out of it together, because I deserve happy, and so do you. We're fucking due, and I fucking love you," he growled, looking so serious that I couldn't help but think that it might actually happen.

With Sterling's determination, and my belief in him, I knew we could make great things.

"I'm scared to have babies," I whispered.

He leaned down and pressed a kiss to my lips, so whisper soft that I barely started getting into it when he pulled back.

"You'll have my babies," he growled.

I laughed at his high handedness.

"Says who?" I asked.

He grinned and maneuvered his body, surprising me when I felt his naked cock pressed against my bare vagina.

Then, with little to do, he slid inside me to the hilt, and I remembered why I would have his babies.

Because he had the most perfect cock in the freakin' world, *that's* why!

I groaned and lifted my hips, pressing my heels into the bed to allow me the extra range of motion that would allow him to reach deeper inside of me.

He didn't like me having so much control, though, which was why he lifted my legs over his shoulders and started to shuttle inside of me.

"Missed you," he breathed against my lips.

"Missed you more," I replied back.

Thrust.

Retreat.

Thrust.

Retreat.

"Love you," I breathed.

He growled.

He bucked when I said those words, and suddenly we were both coming.

Weeks of no sex, compounded with both of our desperation, had both of our orgasms barreling into us and taking us up, up, up, until we couldn't breathe.

"Jesus," Sterling groaned as he spurted deep inside of me.

"Yes!" I agreed.

"Take me. All of me," he ordered.

Always so high handed!

"Yes, sir," I acquiesced.

He laughed into my mouth as our breathing returned to normal, our orgasms so sweet that I was smiling.

"What's with that smile," he asked. "You look evil."

I snorted and he pulled back, his cock slipping from me and leaving me bereft.

"If I was evil, I would say how amazing it felt to have sex with my stepbrother," I teased.

He laughed.

Full, belly roaring, laughed.

"Don't say that anymore," he said. "Not in public, anyway."

"You know you like it," I whispered, eyes getting heavy.

"Yeah, see how much you like it when our friends hear that shit!" He challenge as he started towards the bathroom.

I snorted.

"How do you like the new house?" I asked, the question that'd been on my mind since we'd gotten home and he'd gone to talk with Silas.

"Like it," he said. "But we'll need to go to look at houses soon. It's not big enough."

My brows furrowed.

It was two bedrooms with an office.

Why would he need something bigger?

"What? Sterling," I said, getting out of bed and following him into the bathroom. "It's two bedrooms with an office. What's the reason for more room?"

"I have plans for babies to fill up those rooms…" he said as he bent over to wash his face.

I admired his bare ass and the way the muscles bunched and unclenched.

My mouth watered, and I turned on the shower so I wouldn't jump his bones again.

He had to be tired, and I didn't want to wear him out too much on his first night home.

I'd have to work him back into shape before I expected much more from him.

"Well, then we'll start looking, but it's kind of hard to do anything without you here. I have no credit to speak of, and you disappear at the drop of a hat. We'll need to find someone willing to work with us," I said as I stepped into the shower.

Water started to pour down over my hair, wetting it down until it was slicked back all the way.

Once I was done, I opened my eyes, then screamed to find Sterling standing directly in front of me.

"Shit!" I gasped, hand going over my heart as it galloped away in my chest.

"You're being exceptionally good natured about my job. Are you sure you're okay with it?" He asked.

I nodded. "It's your job. Your passion. What else would I be *but* accepting? I love you. That means you. All of you. Your job. Your stupid quirks about not leaving the towels on the towel bar. You not picking up your things. Everything about you, I love. Even your job."

"So you'll be okay if I leave every couple of months for a job without any notice? You'll get home one day from work and I'll just be gone?"

He pushed.

I nodded again.

I mean, it would suck balls, but I'd get over it.

As long as it made Sterling happy, I was there for him.

Through thick and thin.

He was it for me.

"Yeah, I'll be able to handle it."

He moved forward quickly and gathered me into his arms.

My back met the cool tile of the shower and I gasped.

"Sterling," I squawked, arching forward.

He laughed, then slammed his mouth down on mine.

"Good."

"Well, now that I know you're in a good mood...we need to talk about your mother," I said, touching on the subject that I knew had been bothering him since we'd gotten home.

He sighed and dropped his forehead down on mine.

"What about her?" He whined.

"You need to talk to her."

"I don't want to talk to her," he said.

I sighed.

"You need to. At least to find out why she did what she did. There may be more to the story...plus, you need to find out about those letters," I said carefully. "Find out what happened. Because if she tried to touch base with you, you have something going on that has nothing to do with her."

He stiffened, then his eyes were on mine.

"You think someone took the letters?" He asked slowly.

I shrugged. "Why else wouldn't they have gotten to you?"

His jaw clenched.

"Shit."

"Yeah, *shit*."

CHAPTER 20

I hate you, and then I love you. It's like want to kick you in the balls, then kiss them better for you.
-Ruthie to Sterling

Sterling

"What are you doing?" Garrison asked me.

"He's about to fuck a cop up, which is why I'm with him," Loki said, sounding slightly annoyed.

I grinned at him.

"What makes you think I'm going to fuck her up?" I asked.

He gave me a look that said he wasn't dumb, nor was he going to believe my nonchalant act.

"Because you flipped out on me this morning when you asked where Thomasina lived. And when I wouldn't tell you, you yelled at me," Loki said dryly. "Then you found out anyway."

That was true.

I'd done my research with Garrison.

And the only thing we could come up with as to why the letters weren't delivered to me since we were the ones who were made to go get the mail was that one of us would've taken them.

Our foster father was not only lazy, but refused to do anything he didn't have to do.

That included cleaning the kitchen. Walking his dogs. Washing the trucks. Mowing the lawn. *Getting the fucking mail.*

Getting the mail, though, was one of the easier jobs, and usually given to Thomasina.

So after Garrison and I got to talking this morning, after Ruthie left for her shift, (and I had to admit that I liked being that close to Garrison without actually being in the house) we realized that there really was only one person that would've been able to slip letters out of the mail without us realizing it.

Thomasina.

Hence, why I was now walking up the pathway of her house after receiving the information from Silas, who'd been able to look into his secret database. One that no one ever knew how or why he had.

"I've had enough trouble from her over the years…it's time to clear the air," I said stiffly, raising my fist and pounding on her door.

I didn't have to wait long.

Thomasina answered the door within moments.

Surprisingly, she looked good.

Really good.

I'd only ever seen her in her police uniform over the past ten years.

Seeing her in yoga pants and a cute t-shirt reaffirmed the position that she was, indeed, a female and not a ball busting cop who tried to appear less female in a male world.

Then she spoke, and all thoughts about her being feminine fled.

"What the fuck are you doing here, fucker?" She growled, narrowing her eyes into slits.

I didn't waste time beating around the bush.

"Did you steal my letters from my mother?" I asked, crossing my arms across my chest.

She blinked, then looked down at her feet.

"He told me to," she whispered.

We all knew who 'he' was.

The question was, was that what would he have done to make her do it.

I knew Thomasina wasn't the type to blindly do something.

I knew she was a good cop.

I also knew that my irrational hatred for her wasn't felt by other people. Only me and Garrison…and Cormac.

So I knew she was a good person.

Knew that she wouldn't have done it if she wasn't provoked.

I just wanted to know why.

And where the fuck my letters were…if there were any letters at all.

Taking the word of someone else wasn't my thing.

I had to see the real thing with my own eyes, and right then, I knew that the letters were real, even if Thomasina had taken them.

"Why didn't you tell me?" I asked.

She looked down at her hands.

"There are things a man can do to a woman that don't show scars, Sterling," she finally answered.

It felt like a lead anchor had been dropped in my gut.

No.

NO!

"Fuck me," Garrison whispered somewhere behind me.

I studied Thomasina.

Realized precisely when she was herself.

The nice little girl who followed us around.

And knew the instant that foster father of ours had gotten to her.

"You could've told us," I said gruffly.

Her eyes turned up, and the vulnerability there was staggering.

"You never knew that I knew you were beaten," she whispered. "You always thought I was jealous. And in a way, I was. Just not jealous of you 'spending time with him.' I was jealous of you getting beaten…and me getting…what I got."

My eyes closed and I realized my monumental mistake.

So huge that I didn't think I'd ever be able to make it up to her.

"God, I'm sorry, Thomasina. I wish I'd known. I would've done something," I whispered.

Garrison was suddenly at my side, and I moved to let him speak his peace.

And it was then I realized that the two of them had had some sort of relationship.

Whatever that may consist of.

And maybe Cormac had known they had something, and he was mad at her for hurting Garrison. I made a mental note to ask him about it later.

"The real question is, is after all that we shared, why the hell you couldn't tell me something like that," he asked roughly.

I moved back, not worried about the letters any longer.

They needed some privacy, and I needed room to think.

"Where are you going?" Loki asked.

"To The Clubhouse. I need some time to think."

***

Three hours and a fifth of whiskey later, I was fucking blitzed.

Then again, there were six men drinking with me, and they were all blitzed just as much as I was.

It'd turned into somewhat of a *'glad you're home and not dead'* party with the rest of the Dixie Wardens.

We'd also somehow migrated from the clubhouse to Halligans and Handcuffs.

I vaguely remembered moving in a truck, but I'd not stopped drinking my whiskey the entire time.

At some point Ruthie had shown up for work, taken one look at me, and had shook her head.

She'd been around, but not *around*.

And it was starting to get on my nerves.

"Where's my woman?" I finally asked.

Loki was on the bench next to me.

"With mine. They're talking about all that evil stuff that women talk about," Loki answered.

"They're talking about babies," Sebastian said from my other side.

I looked over at him.

"He did say evil," I told him.

He laughed.

"My kids are evil," he agreed. "But I wouldn't trade them for Trance's kids."

"Hey!" Trance said from the other side of the bar. "They only did that one thing once."

The 'one thing' he was talking about was Trance's son lighting the table on fire.

He'd been playing with a lighter that Trance had thought was empty.

Turns out it wasn't, and he'd lit the tablecloth on fire, which then had taken the old wood table underneath it with it.

Trance and his brothers had carried the table outside and had then watched it burn.

"That's nothin'," Cleo said. "My wife told me about Torren's kid getting into that butt paste shit and smearing it all over their new couch. They had to throw it away."

"That was true," Torren said. "It was a two thousand dollar couch, and since the ass cream is water resistant, there was nothing we could do to get it up. And my kid used the industrial sized tub, meaning it covered the entire couch...and wall...and coffee table...and area rug," he laughed. "But I didn't like the area rug, so it wasn't that big of a bad thing for me."

Torren was sitting behind the bar, directly in front of me, so I could see the evil smile on his face.

"If I didn't know you better, I'd say that you gave that cream to him to do that with," I said.

He shrugged.

"Mebbe'," Torren said. "Backfired like a bitch, though."

I couldn't help it...I laughed.

Hard.

"What are you laughing at?" A woman's voice said from my back.

My woman.

My heart.

My love.

My fucking soul.

"That's sweet," she whispered. "But your friends are looking at you like you're crazy."

I hadn't realized I'd said that out loud.

Oops.

"You done yet?" I asked.

She nodded. "Got done about two minutes ago. You ready to go?"

I nodded. "Yeah. Seems I have to go see my mother tomorrow."

And go kill my foster father.

"You can't go kill anyone," she said. "Just like I told you with my ex's father. Killing them means jail time and dishonorable discharge. Can't have your pretty ass in the prison system. It'd get too worn out."

I grabbed a hold of her hair.

"Nobody will get near my ass," I told her.

She laughed.

"Honey, I'm pretty sure you'd let me do anything, even if it involved your pretty ass."

I growled at her.

The men around me laughed.

Fuckers.

"Let's go home," I ordered.

She snorted. "It should prove fun."

"Why?"

"You'll see."

***

"Help me out!" I yelled for the fourth time.

She'd somehow shoved me into her tin can of a piece of shit car, and I was stuck.

Really fucking stuck.

"You're not stuck, so quit your bitchin'," she growled, opening the door that I couldn't manage to get open.

I fell out, catching myself before my face hit the ground outside our rented house.

"Help me!" I whined, lowering myself down to the ground and laying my hot face against the cool grass.

When no help was forthcoming, I rolled over and stared up at my soon to be wife.

She was so fuckin' beautiful.

And sexy.

"What are you looking at?" I asked her.

She hissed at me. "Shh!"

I blinked, sitting up to see where she was staring, and gasped.

"No!" I bellowed. "Don't do it!"

The two people across the street sprung apart like they'd been cattle prodded.

Thomasina and Garrison had been in each other's arms…seconds away from making a huge mistake.

"You're step sister and step brother!" I yelled.

Ruthie started laughing.

"They are not. They're foster brother and sister. We are the nasty ones, step brother!" She laughed, kicking me lightly in the side.

I thought about that for a few long moments, then nodded my head.

"Okay, y'all may proceed!" I yelled.

Ruthie snorted a laugh, then helped haul me to my feet.

"Goodnight!" I yelled at the pair that were staring at me like I'd grown horns. "I'm going to make some babies with my soon to be wife!"

Ruthie's peals of laughter followed us inside.

And we *did* make a baby.

Mostly because I had told her to stop taking the birth control and she had.

I didn't realize it'd happen so soon, though.

CHAPTER 21

I hope you get a mosquito bite between your toes.
-Ruthie to Sterling

Ruthie

"You look a little green," I said, trying hard not to smile.

"That's because I'm fucking hung over," he growled.

"You were the one to set up this time. Why didn't you just reschedule?" I asked.

"Because I didn't think that it'd be that bad," he answered.

"Sterling," I said slowly. "You drank a fifth of whiskey all by yourself. What'd you think was going to happen? And the sad thing about it all was that you drunk dialed your mother and not me. I mean…who does that?"

"I used to be able to do that and wake up and run five miles the next morning," he grumbled.

I snorted.

"When you were what, eighteen?" I asked. "And you still ran today."

"I ran down the road and had to walk back. That's what took me so long," he confided.

I closed my eyes and smiled as I thought about that.

"I'm sure they'll understand if you want to reschedule," I hesitated. "Although, last night, you kept going on and on about how excited your mother was to speak to you."

"Shit," he sighed. "Let's just get this over with."

He bailed out of the car, and we started walking up the front walk of a huge house that Able had told me he'd rented for the time being.

They usually lived in South Dakota, but had taken up temporary residence here for the summer in what originally had been an attempt to get closer to me.

And was now an attempt to get closer to the both of us.

"There are kids watching us," I whispered to him.

He looked up, and it was freaky as hell to see kids that had both of our features.

"You know," he said under his breath. "That's what our kids are going to look like."

I nodded.

It really was weird.

The kids had my gray eyes, but Sterling's dirty blonde hair.

Sterling's nose, my dimpled butt chin.

"We must've gotten all of our features from our parents," I surmised.

"Yeah," he said. "Jesus Christ, look at the girl."

The girl was smiling, and she had my smile down to a T.

"Oh my God," I whispered. "How are we ever going to explain this off to our friends?"

"We're going to have to move to Arkansas," he teased.

I slapped his arm.

"Shut up!" I laughed as we arrived at the door.

The boy opened the door before we even made it to the door to knock.

He swung it open wide.

"Hi," he said.

"Hi," we both replied back.

"Are you my brother and sister?" He asked.

We both nodded.

"God, you're real," a woman said from beyond the door.

We both moved our eyes from the little boy in front of us to the woman standing behind him.

She was in what I would call the entryway to the entrance.

The room was freakin' massive, like one of those ones you'd see on HGTV's Dream House.

I was scared to step on the carpet, it was that nice and extravagant.

And they were renting this place?

"Come in, come in," the woman rushed out, pulling her smaller son's hand so he backed up so we could make our way inside.

Able appeared in the doorway and my heart skipped a beat at the sight of him.

He was really intimidating, and I saw now how he worked as an independent contractor for the US Government.

He probably only had to show his face and the people were scared to fuck with him.

Not that Sterling was any less intimidating; he just knew how to turn that 'power' as I liked to call it, off.

He could talk to damn near anybody.

Stranger on the street.

An old lady in the grocery store.

The teller at the bank.

Able, though, looked like the type of person that people ran away from.

"Glad y'all could make it," Able said in his deep voice.

I smiled shyly at him.

"Would y'all like something to drink?" The woman asked.

"No thank you, Mrs. Spiers. We just got done eating at Whataburger," I answered.

I almost brought my drink in, but I was pretty sure that the house might fall down around my ears if I brought a fast food cup into it.

"Oh, I made lunch. Oh well, there's dessert!" She cried, turning around to head to the kitchen.

Sterling and I stayed frozen in the entrance, both too scared to follow.

"Did she think we were eating here?" I asked Able.

He shrugged. "Call her Ann Marie, and yes, she thinks everyone that comes to our home is hungry."

Sterling's hand tightened on mine, and I looked up at him.

"What?" I asked.

He shook his head, his eyes looking pointedly at the two kids in front of us.

"What're y'all's names?" He asked them.

"Dalia," the little girl answered.

"Dylan," the boy answered.

"How old are y'all?" I asked.

"I'm ten," Dylan answered. "And Dalia is twelve."

"Cool," Sterling said. "What was for lunch?"

"Tuna fish," Dylan answered. "Even though we all hate it."

I blinked.

I wasn't very fond of it either, but if I had to venture a guess, the tuna fish was for Sterling's benefit.

He loved it and ate it like it was the best thing on earth.

Something about it being healthy, filling, and cheap.

But whatever.

His mother must've remembered how much Sterling liked it, because she made it even though the rest of them disliked it.

Which said something.

I gestured to the kitchen with my eyes; Sterling sighed, taking the hint.

He moved past us, and I admired his ass as he walked stiffly past me.

"Daddy, she's watching his butt. I thought you said they were our brother and sister," Dylan said, sounding amusingly confused.

I rose an eyebrow at Able, wondering how he'd explain that to them.

I smiled when he didn't know what to say.

"Sterling and I are getting married," I said. "And I happen to like looking at his butt."

***

Sterling

The nerves that'd been crawling around in my belly like a nest of agitated snakes became even worse when I walked into the kitchen to find my…mother…putting away what she'd made.

"I like tuna fish. Thank you for making it. Wish I'd known that you were making it," I said softly from the doorway.

My mother's shoulders hunched and she whirled around, the Tupperware in her hands as she finished securing the lid onto it.

"I know you like it," she smiled.

She looked just like I'd remembered.

Long wavy blonde hair the color of the Galveston beach we'd gone to one summer when I was young.

Eyes bright green and shining with…love.

Beautiful white smile.

Long, elegant fingers.

She was slim.

Not even an inch bigger after two more kids.

"I'm sorry," I said finally.

She frowned.

"Sorry for what?" She asked.

"Sorry I didn't get a hold of you earlier," I said.

I could've spoken with her months ago…but I hadn't.

I'd been that poor, scared kid again as he watched his mother walk away from him.

As he watched life as he'd known it end.

A tear slipped out of the corner of one eye and she smiled sadly at me.

"It was me who messed up, son. It's always been me. I couldn't make good decisions to save my life, and you were the one who suffered because of it," she said solemnly.

I shrugged.

"And from what I understand, you didn't get into any better of a situation after I left you. So I didn't win, and I could see why you never answered my letters," she said softly.

I shook my head. "I didn't answer your letters because I didn't get them. My foster father…" I didn't want to say anything about Thomasina. She'd suffered enough at that monster's hands. She didn't need any more scrutiny. "He wasn't a good man. Never saw a single one of the letters that came there."

She frowned.

"I personally delivered two to that man…" she said. "Delivered money there, too. Every time I'd ask about you, he'd say you didn't want to see me."

My jaw clenched.

"He was a piece of shit that deserves to fuckin' die," I growled, eyes going far away as I dreamed about all the ways I could kill him.

"Sterling, darling," she said. "Don't you do what I see dancing in your eyes. He's not worth it."

I crossed my arms over my chest as I watched my mother, the woman who'd been stolen from me by my foster father.

"You don't know me that well," I said defensively.

She laughed.

"Oh, honey. I was the one to diaper your bottom. Hold you in my arms when you were born. I saw you through the chicken pox, pneumonia, your first steps, potty training, your first broken bone, your first lost tooth," she smiled fondly. "And a mother never forgets, trust me. She knows when her child is thinking devious thoughts. Just like I knew you were here, and why I pushed Able to come meet his daughter. Two birds with one stone."

My mouth dropped open.

"You knew I was here all along?" I asked.

She nodded.

"I was there the day you graduated high school. The day you went to prom with Lizzette Boreguard. The day you graduated from boot camp. I'm very proud of you," she whispered.

I blinked.

"Does your husband know all this?" I asked carefully.

She smiled a secret smile at me.

"My husband doesn't know everything about me."

I shook my head.

"I thought you forgot about me."

Tears instantly filled her eyes.

"I'd never forget about you. You were my first baby," she whispered fiercely. "Not one day passed that I didn't cry for you. But I didn't know what else to do. I just kept digging myself deeper and deeper, and pretty soon I couldn't see the light at the end of the tunnel anymore. I just wanted you to be happy...and safe."

My eyes drifted closed, and only opened when I felt my mother's warm embrace pulling me into her.

"I love you, Sterling. Always have, always will."

I coughed to cover up the emotion roiling through me.

"I'm marrying Ruthie," I told her.

My mother leaned back and placed her hands on my cheeks.

"I can't wait to have grandchildren," she said enthusiastically.

I smiled.

"Hopefully that'll come sooner rather than later."

She leaned up and kissed me on the cheek.

"Now, how about you introduce me to your fiancé."

So I did what my mother asked of me.

I introduced her to *my* Ruthie.

***

Later that night

"I need you to give me everything you have on Pete Sorbet," I said to Silas later that evening.

Ruthie was asleep in the bed on the opposite end of the house, and I knew that if I didn't go take care of this, I wouldn't sleep.

It had to happen.

"I'll come get you, you can follow me," he answered instantly.

I smiled.

Pete Sorbet wouldn't know what hit him.

And he had some penance to pay.

Thomasina, Cormac, Garrison, my mother, and I deserved it.

CHAPTER 22

Powered by bitchdust.
-Car Decal

Ruthie

One month later

"I never wanted to be here, doing this. I wanted to sit in those stands right there," Sterling pointed to the spot next to me from his spot near the batter's circle, "and cheer Cormac on. I wanted him to see me sitting there encouraging him, and know that he had love and support. Something we didn't have when we were growing up. It was the Three Musketeers. Us against the world."

A tear slipped down my cheek.

"So I'm going to try out, because I know that's what he always wanted to do. I'm going to fulfill each and every item on his bucket list with our other best friend, Garrison. I'm going to hit that home run that'll shatter all kinds of records. Garrison and I are going to go mountain climbing, even though we're both scared of heights. Because Cormac deserved to live longer than he did, and for that I'll try my hardest to do everything he wanted to do, and live my life the way he wanted me to live it."

Sterling handed the microphone back to the reporter, whose face showed tears just as I had on mine.

Just as everyone in the entire stadium had.

I was sure he hadn't meant for that to go to the entire stadium, and if he'd been thinking a little more clearly he would've noticed how his face was on the huge screens sporadically placed throughout the stadium.

But he wasn't in the best state of mind.

He was somewhere he never wanted to be...at least not for this reason, anyway.

I smiled as he took a couple practice swings.

"Little tight," Garrison called. "Loosen it up."

Garrison and he had been working for this day for a few good weeks, now.

They'd hated every minute of it, not having Cormac there with them, but they knew how important this had been to Cormac, so they did it anyway.

Even though it tore them apart.

"Number 10, Sterling Waters, is the next batter," the announcer said from his perch up high above our heads.

Every last one of Sterling's entourage sat forward in anticipation.

The pitcher threw a couple practice throws, as he, too, was trying out.

And Sterling watched with a practiced eye.

"He's pitching from the stretch," Garrison whispered.

"What does 'pitching from the stretch' mean?" Baylee asked just as quietly from somewhere behind me.

"It means he's not pitching from the wind up," Garrison said distractedly.

I rolled my eyes.

Like that meant a freakin' thing to her!

I would have to explain it to her.

Later.

Because my man, in his tight white baseball pants that were tucked neatly underneath his knees, exposing his bright red socks, was up to bat.

"He looks mean," I whispered.

"That's 'cause he *is* mean," Torren said from behind me.

I didn't rise to the bait.

He really liked to pull my tail.

Instead, I kept my eyes on Sterling.

He was so focused, and unbelievably still.

The red helmet he was wearing shielded his eyes from me, but I knew they were on the ball.

He was watching, taking in the pitcher's movements.

The first ball that was thrown went directly into the catcher's glove, landing with a solid thud.

"Strike," the unofficial ump said.

Sterling didn't fight that call.

We both knew it was a strike.

The next two pitches were balls.

The fourth pitch, though, was *the one.*

The one that was in Sterling's sweet zone.

Thrown exactly where he wanted it.

He swung for the fence.

Fucking yacked it so freakin' hard that the wooden bat split.

Pieces of wood went flying as the bat connected with the ball so perfectly that everyone's inhalation was heard throughout the stadium.

He hit the ball so hard it sailed over not only the wall, but out of the *entire freakin' stadium.*

Then proceeded to hit a ground ball to center field.

A solid hit down the line.

And one more home run.

Needless to say, the scouts were impressed.

***

Sterling

"Can't believe how far you've come when me and dad found you eating out of those trashcans," Sebastian said, pounding me on the back.

"I've told you a million times, I wasn't eating out of the trashcans, I only made it look like that so y'all would leave me alone," I grumbled darkly.

Sebastian's eyes sparkled with mirth.

"And how'd that work out for you?" He asked, punching me in the shoulder.

I immediately returned the punch with just as much force, if not more.

"It didn't," I laughed.

Sebastian had been my sponsor into The Dixie Wardens MC.

He'd changed my life.

And I could never thank him enough.

That night, I'd been trying to break into a veterinarian's office to try to get some medication for Garrison, who'd been sicker than a dog.

Which was apt, I thought, since I'd been breaking into a vet's office.

It still amazed me, how far I'd come.

The Dixie Wardens had changed my life.

They'd been the reason Garrison, Cormac, and I had gotten out of that helacious life.

They'd helped send Garrison to college.

They'd helped get Cormac a job.

And they'd helped me get into the Navy, and watched over my brothers while I'd been gone.

If you'd asked me ten years ago, I would never have thought I'd be in this position, with the opportunity of a lifetime sitting in my lap.

"So, are you going to take it?" Sebastian finally asked, offering me a beer.

I'd been offered a place on the minor league team for the Shreveport Spark's, with a chance to move up to the Major League's if I had enough drive.

Something I knew I could accomplish.

But being on a major league team had never been my dream.

It'd been Cormac's.

I'd never thought that I'd make it.

I'd thought I'd get here, try out, and be sent home.

Never in a million years would I have thought this day would've gone this way.

"I don't know," I said truthfully. "I need to talk to my girl."

Sebastian pounded me lightly on the shoulder, and I watched as my wife to be walked to me from across the room.

We were at Halligan's and Handcuffs.

She wasn't working today since we'd taken the day so she could come to the tryouts.

Now we were at the bar, celebrating the fact that the Spark's actually wanted me. A man that was nearly twenty-seven and hadn't played baseball competitively in a very long time.

Well, I was drinking.

Ruthie wasn't.

That was because Ruthie was pregnant.

Even though she was still in denial with the news.

We'd thrown out her birth control pills nearly six weeks ago.

Well I had, Ruthie had just gone with the flow.

She had to have known it'd happen.

"You okay?" She asked me, wrapping her hands around me.

I shrugged.

"I always thought it'd be me who died first. I was the one with the dangerous job. I was the one who put my life on my line. Not him. He was only playing baseball. How could this happen to him and not me?" I asked her.

Ruthie's eyes filled with tears, and they slipped over as she leaned forward and placed her lips against mine.

"I don't know. Life is unpredictable. You never know what you're going to get. We can't see into the future and we can't change the past. You'll just have to learn to live with it, and hope you have someone like me and your friends, *your brothers*, to see you through," she said softly.

I groaned.

"I don't know what to do," I admitted.

I was so torn.

On one hand I knew what kind of opportunity this was.

Knew that if I did this, this could mean huge things for Ruthie and me.

We could have so many things that my job as a Navy SEAL wouldn't offer us.

But I loved being a SEAL.

Loved my team.

"This is completely up to you," she whispered. "And I'll be with you every step of the way."

"As will we, my man," Sebastian said.

I hadn't realized he was still there.

But he was.

And I was okay with him hearing all that was just said.

"So you're saying I can still be a Dixie Warden if I'm a professional baseball player?" I teased. "There's not some secret code against that?"

He snorted. "There's not a rule book on how to be a biker. No one said you can't do what you want to do. And if baseball is what you want to do, then fuckin' do it."

"Yeah," Kettle said, plopping down on the bar stool beside us. "'Cause you know how I like good seats."

"You don't even like baseball," Adeline said, wrapping her hands around her husband's neck from behind.

Kettle shrugged. "I do when there's beer involved. I can handle anything when there's beer."

We laughed.

And we were happy.

The woman I loved was at my side.

We had a child on the way.

And I knew that, somewhere in heaven, Cormac was smiling down at me.

Silently urging me closer and closer to the life I was meant to live.

As a husband.

A father.

A member of The Dixie Wardens MC.

And a motherfucking professional baseball player.

EPILOGUE

Dear Lord,
Thank you for baseball pants.
Amen
-Ruthie's secret thoughts

Sterling

Seven months and fifteen days later

"You're up, Waters," Coach said, slapping me hard on the right shoulder.

I shrugged off the pain and jogged to the bats, picking up my favorite.

Each player had their own bat, and it'd been a real eye opener to me when I'd been given option after option of what type of equipment I could use.

I tucked the bat under my arm as I walked up the steps, multitasking by slipping my hands into my batting gloves as I did.

"You ready?" The batting coach, Lou Jacobs, asked.

I nodded.

I was ready.

This would be my thirty third major league baseball game.

I'd started out in the minor leagues, proving myself to all those involved.

Once I'd done that, I was called up to the majors, where I rode the bench for two months before I was ever put in.

But once I was, I'd proven myself.

My first at bat, I'd hit a line drive to center field.

It'd bounced off the wall and given me my first ever double as a professional baseball player.

That'd been the day that everything became 'real.'

Every day I missed the life I used to have.

But I still had my family.

My friends.

My Teams.

Yes, I said *teams*.

I was still a member of SEAL Team 11, as well as the first baseman for The Shreveport Spark's.

Not that I did any more missions.

Things had taken a drastic turn for SEAL Team 11 when the rest of the world had been made aware of just how much bullshit the team had been placed under with the fucktard and the fucktard's pregnant ex-wife.

A pregnant ex-wife who'd *wanted* to be with who she was with, and had resorted to calling the media about her controlling ex-husband who wouldn't take 'no' as an answer when she realized that he wasn't going to stop.

The second mission we'd been sent on to bring the senator's ex-wife home had been eye opening, and the team had learned from the ex-wife and the new lover that the man wouldn't leave them alone, which was why they'd moved out of the country in the first place.

After awareness was made on both parts, our captain had pulled us out, much to the senator's frustration.

The dumbass had then tried to throw the entirety of SEAL Team 11 under the bus, but with the help of Silas, as well as a few other government officials, that had backfired on him.

He was screwed, and SEAL Team 11 was now *America's team.*

Especially since all of our identities were revealed, rendering our ability to go on missions safely invalid.

Which was also why I hadn't worried about being public 'face.'

America thought it was awesome that a SEAL was playing for the Shreveport Sparks.

They thought it was so cool, in fact, that the newest team in the MLB had an instant fan base overnight.

"Get your head in the game, boy."

I winced at my coach's apt words.

My head wasn't in the game.

It was in my other life.

The one I had when I wasn't playing baseball.

"Yes, sir," I said, taking a few practice swings and testing the weight of the bat.

It was the first base coach that had the adrenaline really shooting through my body, though.

"Your wife called, she's in labor," Coach Dennis said.

"Fuuuuck," I said, not knowing what to do.

My eyes moved up to the stands to where all of my 'family' had permanent seats, and I could tell right off the bat that Ruthie wasn't lying.

I could see her hunched over her round belly with her teeth gritted.

But she managed a small wave that let me know she was staying till the end.

"Shit," I said, turning back around.

"Just bring it in, and you can go," the coach said from my back.

I took a few lead off steps, resisting the urge that practically screamed for me to go to Ruthie, and watched the batter.

We'd discussed the possibilities of this happening.

When I'd made the suggestion that she stay home today after hearing she was experiencing contractions, she'd looked at me like I was nuts.

But I couldn't really refuse Ruthie anything.

She could talk me into just about anything without much of an effort.

Luckily, Sebastian sat on one side of her, Kettle on the other, and Cleo was directly behind them.

I knew she was in good hands.

That still didn't make the next two at bat's any less painful.

The first hitter, Consuelo, knocked the ball down the third base line.

I moved to second with my heart in my throat, resisting the urge to run for third.

Years and years of patience had me viciously locking that desire down until the next batter, Gonzales, came up.

Gonzales bunted, and while they were busy trying to get him out, I not only hit third, but I hit home base as well, surprising not just the opposite team's players, but the whole stadium as well.

The coach just gave me a roll of the eyes as I ran up to the dugout and started tugging off my helmet.

"I gotta go," I said urgently.

He nodded. "That's fine. You just won the game, anyway."

I probably did, but it was up to my team to shut it down completely in the next three innings.

"Thanks," I said, hurrying down the field.

I jumped the fence that sat directly in front of my family, and dropped down to one knee in front of my wife.

"Ready?" I asked.

I could see that her water had broken.

But she just sat there, as patient as could be, waiting for me to arrive.

"Yep. Let's do this."

Then, to the fan's delight, I carried my woman out of the stadium.

***

I picked up the soft, pale yellow body suit, and smiled before tossing it into the dirty clothes hamper by the cleanest corner.

It was the same body suit that Ruthie had picked out for her little Jade to wear home from the hospital.

We'd put it onto Cormac for all of thirty seconds before he'd shit all over it.

He'd had to come home in the hospital's white shirt that declared him a 'Superstar.'

Which had chapped Ruthie's ass something fierce.

I'd had to explain to her that it'd be easier to go home with our child rather than sending me home for the outfit that she had for him as a backup.

Something I'd mistakenly taken home with me earlier in the afternoon when I was trying to help out.

Now we were all home, and our house was filled to the brim with family.

Silas and Sawyer.

Sebastian and Baylee.

Kettle and Adeline.

Viddy and Trance.

Loki and Channing.

Rue and Cleo.

Tru and Torren.

My mom. Ruthie's dad.

Our brother and sister.

Dixie.

Garrison.

Thomasina.

Lily, Dante, and their two children.

And many, many more.

There were so many people that they'd had to spill out on the back deck.

But I wouldn't change it for the world.

"Here, hold him for a second, would you?" Ruthie asked as she yanked her shirt down and exposed her breasts.

My eyes widened, and my cock instantly got hard.

But that was the way it was with my Ruthie.

It didn't matter that she'd just pushed out a baby the size of a small house.

Lani Lynn Vale

Her breasts weren't affected, and my cock didn't seem to care that they were now going to go hand in hand with our son for the next year.

All it cared about was the fact that it hadn't had any of Ruthie for well over a week.

The small ball of life in my arms made a grunting sound before he started to wail his little lungs, making the sweetest sound that I'd ever heard.

"Will you change him?" She asked.

I winced.

I'd yet to do that.

I was scared to break him.

"I guess," I said reluctantly.

She snorted as she worked a shirt on over her breasts.

A breast-feeding tank that would give her easier access to Cormac's milk supply.

"Hurry up," she laughed. "We have a house full of people."

That we did.

So I opened the door carefully that would lead into the hallway, then continued down to Cormac's room.

This place was a baseball lover's dream.

Signed balls lined shelves.

The walls were painted to resemble a baseball field.

The bedding was white with the red stitching of a baseball.

Seriously, every kid in their right mind would love this room.

Hell, after seeing it, I'd wanted to do my own man cave to resemble it.

Which was quickly shot down by Ruthie since she'd made the only other spare room into a sewing room.

Something she'd taken to doing when she quit her job at Halligans and Handcuffs to make up the difference in income.

She was actually doing quite well at it, too.

Not that she needed to.

She just wanted to.

Which was okay with me.

Except for the monogramming.

Every fucking thing Cormac had had his initials, or name, or something cutesy on it.

Poor kid was going to grow up with a complex if she kept it up.

I placed a soft kiss on Cormac's head before I sat him down carefully on the soft changing pad.

I was nearly to his diaper when I was interrupted.

"Got a call today about a certain foster father," Silas said from behind me.

I raised a brow at him, placing my hand on the middle of Cormac's chest to keep him on the changing table while my eyes weren't on him.

"Oh yeah?" I asked nonchalantly.

Silas nodded, coming into the room.

He had his own little girl, Amelia, asleep on his chest.

She was a little over nine months old, and the absolute cutest thing I'd ever seen.

Besides my own child, of course.

Who would've thought that we'd all be having kids together with such an age gap between us all?

"Seems he took a fall in the yard, had to go to the infirmary. Sustained a broken femur, broken hand, fracture to his right eye socket, and a concussion."

"Hmm," I said. "Imagine that."

I made sure to have my good ol' foster father taken care of every few weeks or so.

He healed, and he seemed to have another accident.

He was a klutz, after all.

"And seems John Wait had another setback with his treatment," Silas continued. "He's been given a new medication that makes him nearly comatose when he's on it. It's a thing of beauty."

I smiled at my son as he wiggled around, hating the fact that I'd just exposed his goods to the cool air.

I covered him quickly with the stupid pee-pee tee-pee thing that Ruthie had gotten at her baby shower.

Something I hadn't realized that was needed until I'd watch Ruthie, and my mother, get peed on earlier this morning.

Something I didn't want happening to me, hence why using the tee-pee thing.

"That's a cryin' shame," I said, reaching for the diaper and looking at it.

John Wait was declared clinically insane after he was found guilty murdering Cormac.

And although he said he'd never thought it would go that far as killing her, he'd still cut Ruthie's brakes.

Had still killed my brother.

Which was why I also went out of my way to see that John's medications were changed every couple of weeks, so that he was always going to be 'unwell.'

He wouldn't be getting out of that mental hospital unless it was in a fucking body bag.

Silas reached over my shoulder and said, "This side down."

I hadn't realized I'd been staring at the diaper while I thought about the vile man that'd taken my friend from me.

I followed his direction, putting the tiniest diaper in the world on my kid.

"Tighter," Silas instructed.

"Who would've thought one biker would be giving another biker directions on how to diaper a baby?" An amused female voice said from behind me.

"I've had four kids now. You'd be an idiot not to take advice from me," Silas said as he left.

I smiled down at my boy as Ruthie made her way to us.

She was dressed much more appropriately now, her breasts covered, and a pair of shorts covering her ass.

"All done?" She asked.

I nodded, holding Cormac up for her inspection.

She snorted as she took him from me, curling him into her arms against her breasts.

"You've got a ton of people here," she said. "Why don't you go talk to them while I order pizza?"

I didn't.

Instead, I pulled her into my arms and pressed my lips against her forehead.

"I'm proud of you," I said, so freakin' happy that I could scream it to the world.

She pressed her lips to mine.

"Go," she said again.

I laughed.

"What my wife wants, my wife gets."

***

Ruthie

The next day

"You just had a baby, you can't go to a baseball game. And Cormac's too little to go," my mother in law tried.

I gave her a look as I packed Cormac's diaper bag into the car.

"We'll be fine," I said, picking up Cormac, car seat and all, and placing him in the Tahoe Sterling had bought for me.

Ann Marie sighed.

"Fine, I guess I'll have to go with you," she grumbled.

I laughed.

She actually thought I wasn't going to go to Sterling's game?

I hadn't missed a home game yet, and it wouldn't be happening ever, if I could help it.

My car quickly filled up.

Ann Marie in the back seat next to Cormac. Silas and Sawyer with their daughter took up the remaining seats.

Silas took the front seat, though.

He'd have probably liked to drive there, but parking cost a whack, and we all usually went in as few vehicles as possible since it wasn't unusual for nearly ten people to go at a time.

The seats Sterling had reserved for his family and friends never went unoccupied, and if I had my way, never would.

"Let's ride," Silas ordered.

I snorted at his impatience.

Silas had become Sterling's dad of sorts.

Someone that Sterling would forever look up to, as did most of the Dixie Wardens MC.

"Can't believe you're doing this," Ann Marie said from the backseat.

I could.

And the look on Sterling's face when he saw me in my seats with his son in my arms, was so incredibly worth all the pain it caused me to sit in the most uncomfortable seats in the world for over four hours.

Worth it, indeed, I thought as I blew him a kiss.

A kiss in which he caught.

I love you, I mouthed.

He grinned. *Love you more.*

ABOUT THE AUTHOR

Lani Lynn Vale is married to the love of her life that she met in high school. She fell in love with him because he was wearing baseball pants. Ten years later they have three perfectly crazy children and a cat named Demon who likes to wake her up at ungodly times in the night. They live in the greatest state in the world, Texas. She writes contemporary and romantic suspense, and has a love for all things romance. You can find Lani in front of her computer writing away in her fictional characters world...that is until her husband and kids demand sustenance in the form of food and drink.

Made in the USA
Monee, IL
27 April 2021